CHRISTINE'S MAN

JERRY MUSHIN

First published in Australia in 2020 by Shooting Star Press

PO Box 6813, Charnwood ACT 2615

info@shootingstar.pub www.shootingstar.pub

ABN 63 158 506 524

A catalogue record for this book is available from the National Library of Australia.

ISBN: 978-1-925821-15-4 Print

ISBN: 978-1-925821-16-1 e Book

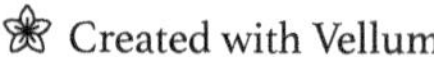 Created with Vellum

TABLE OF CONTENTS

This book is dedicated to the academic and secretarial staff of the Department of Economics at Dunton Polytechnic which, despite having become the University of Duntonshire, has never existed, and to Christine who, although fictitious, has been married to the author for many years.

"A review by the CNAA is an
opportunity for those who
know the truth and wish to
conceal it to give misleading
answers in response to
irrelevant questions asked
by those who suspect the
truth and wish to avoid hearing
it."
—anonymous polytechnic lecturer, 1985

1

———

Bob Morgan stared at the ceiling above his bed. Had it been decorated with rectangular tiles he would have counted them. Since it was covered merely with flaking off-white paint, he had to make do with trying, once again, to find a meaning in the cracks in the plaster. By using a lot of imagination, which some might call creative genius, he managed to find a lop-sided giraffe. By shutting one eye and placing half his thumb in front of the other, however, he discovered the outline of an igloo in need of a refreeze. But, as he frequently asked his economics students at Dunton Polytechnic, what did it mean? Measurement of the facts should never be considered of value without explanation and interpretation. For four years he had been repeating this theme, sometimes even to the point of hectoring his weaker, somnolent students, but was there any point if he could not even apply the principle to the simple matter of ceiling plaster?

With a sudden effort, he sat up in bed, leapt to the floor, sprinted across the lino to the window, opened the curtains to reveal a sunny morning, and hurried back to bed to nurse his cold feet. Bob decided to make a plan of action for the new term. In one week, the new academic year started, and it was as well to be ready, and now was the time to devise plans, while there was still time to think. He started to draw up a mental list. The flat needed painting, and probably replastering too. On the other hand, it hadn't been painted for many years, so a little longer would surely not be critical. Perhaps in sympathy with the condition of the flat, his car was showing geriatric symptoms, but this was more urgent because the annual MOT test was due in a couple of weeks, and a costly failure, even at one of the smaller scruffy garages where they give a discount for settlement in cash rather than by cheque, was almost certain. Even the car problem, though, was not the most pressing worry. His bank manager had provided loans on demand many times, and a car loan might even cover the cost of a bedroom carpet, too. He tried to put money problems out of his mind.

The real problem, Bob decided, as he had decided many times before, was the job. When he had been appointed as a lecturer at Dunton Polytechnic, it had seemed like the answer to all his dreams: interesting work, regular salary, professional status, and something for his mother to boast about. In the event, although he loved teaching, many aspects of the job had turned sour. Even his mother kept complaining that a post at a university would be easier to explain to her doctor, her hairdresser, and her greengrocer.

The main problem of the job was that there was too much to do and not enough time to do it in. "Higher Education on the Cheap" was how some of his colleagues described the polytechnic. Long teaching hours, as many in a week as some university staff might be expected to complete in a term or, so it had been rumoured, even in a year, left him feeling permanently tired. The rapid evolution of syllabuses meant that, even after four years, he did not have an adequate fund of prepared lecture notes. He constantly felt that, with a bit more time, he might be able to do his teaching very well indeed, to the combined satisfaction of his students, himself, and the polytechnic hierarchy. No. Bob decided, having thought these thoughts on many occasions, his ultimate objection was to the non-teaching part of the job. He hated committee meetings, where the real object of many partici- pants was to win, or at least not to lose. He hated the style of his head of department, whose main objective was not to offend the principal of the polytechnic, and he hated the whole process of external validation of courses, where the aim of most of his colleagues was to present favourable impressions of the polytechnic rather than to tell the whole truth.

Bob was suddenly thrown out of his deep thoughts by the shrill ringing of his alarm clock. Once again, Morgan's Law of Mornings had been demonstrated: "The need for an alarm clock varies inversely with the efficiency with which it is set."

There was a sharp clip as the postman pushed some letters through the door and the letter-box snapped shut. Bob picked them up and immediately put a double-glazing adver- tisement into the kitchen bin without opening the envelope. Some problems he could solve easily. The other letters were equally uninteresting. There was one from his mother in which she wrote that the weather was fine (for the time of year) and that she was keeping busy. She always claimed to be busy, which Bob suspected meant that she wasn't, but he had enough worries without taking that one on too. The third letter was a reminder that his next dental check-up was due; no inspiration there, just another reason to worry.

BOB DRESSED, had breakfast, and drove to the polytechnic. Although the new term did not start for a week, most of the teaching staff were there. Some were undertaking academic work such as preparing lecture notes or writing learned theses, but at this time of the year activity was concentrated on administrative matters. Timetabling of classes was always a problem even though the student population did not increase much from one year to the next, the building did not get any smaller, and the number of lecturers did not fall. Every September, and this September would prove to be no exception, small classes were allocated to big rooms (which did not matter) and *vice versa* (which did), classes requiring access to computer facilities were sent to rooms where there were none, multiple classes were allocated to the same room at the same time, and lecturers were told to be in two places at once. Fortunately, Bob thought, that's not my problem, and, to a large extent, he was able to leave it to other unfortunate people, despite their efforts to involve him.

One matter that he could not avoid, because he had been singled out and instructed to deal with it, was the selection of new students. His particular course responsibility was the BA in Economics. Every year the polytechnic received about eighty applications for a total of thirty places on this course, but, every year, most of these applicants enrolled at more prestige institutions of learning, or failed their "A" Level examinations, or switched to other subjects, or found employment, or perhaps even died, emigrated, or went to prison. Whatever the explanation, however, the effect was that every August many places on the course remained unfilled and, to protect the honour of the polytechnic, the jobs of its staff, and the good humour of its principal, these places had to be filled. It was the proudly-declared policy of the polytechnic, though none of the academic staff knew why, that all applicants were interviewed, and this was how Bob was to spend his morning.

Bob entered the main polytechnic building, noted that the queue in front of the lift was four times its capacity, and walked up the stairs to his office on the top floor. It was a small office and was the only one in the department not to have a telephone. The two facts were not unrelated; the architect had intended the room to contain a toilet. The consolation was that he shared with only one other lecturer. His frequent pleas for a telephone to be installed had been ignored and had even, he felt, become a regular ritual, like Guy Fawkes night, whose meaning had been lost.

He walked the thirty yards to the departmental secretary's office to arrange for the candidates to be sent to his office at fifteen-minute intervals (just the moment when a telephone would have been useful!) and then, since it was not yet nine o'clock, he sat down at his desk and waited for the first to arrive.

The first interviewee knocked, and was invited to enter and sit down. Bob asked her why she had chosen Dunton Polytechnic. There was a long silence while she appeared to be counting the lace-holes on his shoes, and then, in a fit of accuracy mania, repeating the measurement again and again.

"Well," she said at last, "I applied to lots of colleges."

Bob then asked her why she had selected the BA in Economics.

This was an easier question.

"My history teacher said the exams in economics are easy."

He asked her what career she hoped to follow after graduating. She did not know. He asked whether she had ever been to Dunton before. She had not. He asked about her leisure pursuits. She had none. He asked whether she was concerned, in view of her fourth-attempt marginal pass in mathematics at "O" level, that the course contained mathematics and statistics as compulsory subjects. She had not noticed this in the course pamphlet. He pointed out that mathematics and statistics were subjects with high failure rates, but she still showed no emotion. After eight minutes, he ended the interview, and the candidate left the room. He recorded the decision that she should be offered a place. The social cost of vacant places was very high, and he had to consider his own happiness at least some of the time.

WHEN BOB GOT home that evening, feeling drained from spending the whole day asking superficial questions to prospective students, many of whom were both bored and boring, he found a note pinned to his front door. "PARCEL AT NO 26" was the message, thus making it obvious that the flat had been empty for much of the day. Fortunately, Dunton's burglars always missed this regular cue.

He collected his parcel. There was the usual reason why the postman had been unwilling to take it back to the sorting office. It contained a home-made fruit pie sent by his mother, and the contents were, as usual, leaking out to form dark wet stains on the brown wrapping paper. Bob held it at arm's length to protect his clothes, and took it home. On the kitchen table he tried to separate the layers of soggy paper from the gift within but, as usual, gave up quickly, and put the whole sticky mess into the dustbin. That evening he spent an hour trying to compose his thankyou letter. He wanted it to be truthful, but not too truthful and, hopefully, different to the others he had written. Eventually, he went out and bought a picture postcard, addressed and stamped it, and then wrote the message: "Some Parcel - Some Mum! (Apologies to Churchill)". His mother was delighted, and started preparing the next weekly consignment ahead of schedule. Bob never dared to ask what his mother thought the message meant. He didn't know himself.

THE DOORBELL RANG while Bob was doing his twice-weekly washing up. He constantly resolved to wash up straight after each meal but was never able to maintain this policy for more than a few days. With only one plate, one cup, and one frying pan to each meal, it never seemed worth doing immediately, and would, in any case, interfere with the post-meal snooze followed by *The Archers* that were essential preparation for an evening of literary activity.

He opened the front door, and old Mrs Lowson's face sprang to smiling attention.

"How are you, my love? Are you tired? Do they keep you busy at your work? You're looking pale; are you run down? I do hope you're eating well. Greens is what you need, plenty of greens. I worry about you, living alone. Anyway, I've brought you a jar of my tomato chutney. I gave most of it to the Sale of Work at the church, but kept the best jar for you. I was going to give it to my cousin Henry, but, well, you know how he is about my chutney, but I know you like it ..."

Bob leaned against the door-post, and waited for her to stop talking. He knew that there would be no point in trying to rush her. It was impossible to swim against such a current. She probably wanted to be invited into the flat for a cup of tea; he had made that mistake only once and it had lasted a whole evening, and only ended when he fell asleep while trying to look attentive.

To Bob's relief the telephone started to ring, so he was able to interrupt Mrs Lowson, wish her well, and close the front door. On his way to the telephone, he placed the jar of chutney in the kitchen cupboard alongside seven similar jars. He didn't like to put the foul-smelling stuff in the dustbin in case he was observed, and there was always the chance that it might be useful, though he had no idea for what.

He picked up the receiver and then sank wearily into an armchair when he realised who was speaking to him. He really did not wish to speak to Eleanor now, or indeed ever again, but he still felt considerable affection for her, so found it impossible to be abrupt.

Eleanor and Bob had met on holiday eight years earlier and, inexplicably, had remained in contact. She now worked as a courier for an American travel firm that specialised in quasi-educational tours for over-indulged children of moneyed parents. She telephoned frequently, from Los Angeles, Miami, Oslo, Rome, Vienna, or wherever her firm sent her. Bob's participation in such telephone conversations was usually limited to occasional grunts while he supported the receiver on a hunched shoulder and concentrated on the Agatha Christie paperback on his lap. This was partly because she spoke so fast, at such length, and with such short pauses for breath, and partly because he no longer had any interest in the domestic arrangements in Nicosia hotels, the intolerance of taxi-drivers in Brussels, the exploitation of restaurant customers in Geneva, or the many other such matters so close to her heart.

Tonight, however, Eleanor was speaking from London, and wanted to visit him in Dunton. He didn't have the energy to argue, so agreed to welcome her the weekend after next. He tried to emphasise that this arrangement was only provisional and semi-definite, but she had already rung off.

Bob was now ready for bed. Another day had passed, and he had spent it solving, or trying to solve, other people's problems. He had even created a new problem in Eleanor's visit. He had been reminded once more that the chutney-mountain was crowding out things that mattered in his kitchen cupboard, and, perhaps most important of all, he had made, in the interests of harmony with his head of department at the polytechnic, a number of decisions that he felt were unsound or, perhaps more properly, unprofessional. Admitting weak students, as instructed, solved the immediate crisis of vacant places, but were, he knew from experience, the seeds from which several years' problems would be harvested.

No progress had been made on his persistent worries of his job, his car, and his flat, to say nothing of Eleanor, his mother's cooking, and Mrs Lowson's chutney. He resolved, yet again, that tomorrow would be the day to plan his campaign.

2

———

Bob entered the polytechnic's Board Room fifteen minutes before the Examination Board meeting was due to start. He wanted to be one of the first to arrive so that he could choose a seat where the majority of board members could see him. At the June meeting, in a mood of end-of-term weariness, he had made only token protests when, on the basis of flimsy excuses, several students who, he felt, should have been required to withdraw from the course had been offered the chance to take resit examinations. Today he intended to take a much more active role. He had decided that the time had come for someone to reassert high standards, and that he was that person. He intended to press the view that students who had failed resit examinations should not be permitted to enter the next year of the course, but he knew it would be a tough battle.

The Board Room gradually filled with lecturers and their heads of department. The secretary distributed copies of a list of the resit candidates and their examination marks. At 9.30 am, when the meeting was scheduled to begin, everyone was present except the chairman and the two external examiners.

External examiners at Dunton Polytechnic were paid substantial sums to monitor the assessment process and, if necessary, to impose decisions. Even a unanimous vote of polytechnic staff at a meeting of an Examination Board could be overruled by either of the external examiners. It was a sad fact, however, that some external examiners took their duties more seriously than others. Newly appointed external examiners would be attending this meeting, and none of the staff knew how they would behave ...

By 9.45 am, when the chairman and external examiners had still not arrived, the assembled lecturers had begun to grumble about their valuable time being wasted. By ten o'clock, when the three seats at the head of the long table were still empty, moans had become caustic jokes. Someone suggested that perhaps the external examiners were being offered drinks. Someone else wondered if bribes were being negotiated. Maybe, came a strident voice from the far end of the room, they're being shown photographs with a view to blackmail ...

At 10.05 am, thirty-five minutes late, the chairman and external examiners entered and took their seats. Suddenly there was silence.

The chairman cleared his throat. "Good morning, gentlemen," he said, and then added, "and ladies of course."

There was a pause. No-one moved. The chairman went on: "I welcome you to this meeting of the Examination Board for the BA in Economics at Dunton Polytechnic. I am particularly pleased to welcome our new external examiners: Professor Basil Blackhurst of the University of Bumstead, and Dr John Nottem of the University of Clamford. We look forward to their contribution to this meeting and, of course, to meetings throughout their term of office."

There was another pause. No-one moved. The chairman

continued: "May I apologise for the lateness of myself and Professor Blockhurst and Dr Nottem; we had some important matters to discuss in private before the start of the meeting."

There was a rumble of grumbles and comments. Many were heard by the chairman whose face reddened. He called the meeting to order: "Gentlemen, please, may we proceed with the meeting? And ladies, of course."

The noise ceased. and the chairman continued: "Apologies for absence? May I take it that there are none?" No-one moved, so the secretary recorded that there were none. "Minutes of the last meeting. May I take it that they are accurate?" No-one moved. Most of those present had not read them, and the rest had forgotten what they said. The chairman waited, and still no-one moved, so the secretary recorded that the minutes had been approved. "Matters arising from the minutes, gentlemen? And ladies, of course." No-one moved. The secretary noted that there were no matters arising.

"And so," said the chairman, "we come to the main business of this meeting: the resit examination results." There was a murmur of approval, and several people sat forward in their seats. Bob, however, was conserving his strength, and remained at ease.

"Let us start with the first-year students," said the chairman, "and I'll take them in alphabetical order. The examination scripts have been checked by the external examiners, and they have not changed any of the marks. OK, then, is everyone paying attention? Andrews, Brown, Cadson, Collins, Davidson, Dawson, and Dobbs have all passed their resit examinations and should be permitted to enter the second year. Is that agreed?" No-one moved, which meant that it was.

"The next candidate is Evans, who has scored 32% in Economic Theory. Would anyone like to comment?"

Bob put his hand up. "That mark is a failure," he said, "so

I propose that Mr Evans be offered a repeat of the first year of the course."

The chairman looked shocked. "That sounds very harsh, Mr Morgan. Would anyone else like to comment?"

"I can assure you that Evans is a hard-working student," said one of his lecturers, "so I think we should be sympathetic."

"Hear, hear," said the chairman.

"But he's failed," said Bob.

"Can I point out," said another lecturer, "that Evans was ill for a few weeks in January, and I think we should take this into account."

"But it's now September," said Bob, "so that's not relevant. And he's failed at the second attempt."

"Please, Mr Morgan," said the chairman, "you've had your turn."

"His essays were very good," said another lecturer.

"But he's failed the examination twice," said Bob, "and the external examiners agree with the marks awarded." The chairman grimaced at him.

"Economic Theory is a continuing subject," contributed another lecturer, "so I suggest that Evans could continue to study first-year material while attending second-year lectures."

"That's absurd," said Bob, "he has demonstrated that he has not mastered the easier theory, so will not be able to cope with more advanced work."

"The examination regulations do allow us to be flexible, and do specifically state that we can use our discretion in exceptional cases," said the head of department's usual yes-man.

"But you treat every failure as an exceptional case," said Bob.

"Please withdraw that remark, Mr Morgan," said the chairman abruptly. Bob said nothing, and the chairman ignored his silence.

"Well," said the chairman, after another forty minutes of discussion of Mr Evans' examination results, "I think the feeling of the meeting is clear, and I propose that we condone Mr Evans' examination failure, and allow him to proceed to the second year of the course. Is that agreed?"

"No," said Bob, "the student has failed, and there are no mitigating circumstances."

"He was ill," said someone.

"Eight months ago," said Bob, "and he's failed twice."

"He has improved his mark since the June exam," said someone else.

"Yes," said Bob, "but he has still failed."

"He gets very nervous in exams."

"So does everyone else," said Bob.

"He is very hardworking."

"So is Donald Duck," said Bob.

"Just a minute," said the chairman, "who is chairing this meeting?" Bob ignored the taunt. "Can I take it then," continued the chairman, "that we have decided to condone Mr Evans' mark and that therefore he has passed to the second year of the course?"

"No," said Bob, ignoring the chairman's open mouth, "I think we should take a vote."

The chairman disagreed. "That's not our usual practice, Mr Morgan. The chairman is usually permitted to assess the feeling of the meeting."

"I am asking for a vote," said Bob, emphasising every word.

The chairman sighed deeply and pushed his fingers through his hair. "Very well," he said. "May I see those in favour of condoning Mr Evans' failure in the Economic Theory examination, in view of his hard work, his good essays, and his illness?" Bob spluttered at this biased summing-up, but was ignored. Eight votes were recorded. "Those against?" Again eight votes were recorded. The chairman looked suddenly elderly.

Bob seized the initiative. "May we hear from the external examiners?" he said.

There was a pause. "Well," said Professor Basil Blackhurst and Dr John Nottem simultaneously, and then each looked at the other and with a magnanimous gesture invited him to proceed. Neither did so, and it fell to the chairman to resolve the deadlock. "Professor Blackhurst," he said, "could we have your views?"

"Ah, yes," said Professor Blackhurst, "this is a difficult one, a very difficult one."

"No, it isn't," said Bob in a stage whisper.

Professor Blockhurst pretended not to hear. "I think ..." he said, talking very slowly in the hope that he would think of something to say fairly soon, "I think I would be prepared to go along with whatever the polytechnic staff decide."

"Thank you," said the chairman.

"For nothing," whispered Bob loudly.

"Dr Nottem?" said the chairman.

"We must be careful to be absolutely fair," said or Nottem, "and consider each case on its merits. We must not ignore any relevant facts. Discretion is allowed to this Board, but it must not be used excessively. Mitigating circumstances may be taken into account, but only if we are certain that they genuinely occurred, and are equally certain that they are genuinely mitigating. We must beware of creating dangerous precedents. Justice, though, should be tempered with compassion."

Everyone waited, but Dr Nottem had nothing else to say.

The chairman looked as weary as everyone else felt.

"I am going to ask each of the external examiners to express a view on the motion before us," said the chairman. "Professor Blackhurst?"

Professor Blackhurst smiled. "I wish to abstain," he said after a pause.

"What a way to earn a living," whispered Bob.

"Dr Nottem?" said the chairman.

"On balance," said Dr Nottem, "and considering all the views I have heard, in the context of the facts, and in relation to existing practice at other institutions of higher education in the United Kingdom, I support the proposal of Mr Morgan."

The meeting exploded into simultaneous cheering and booing, and the chairman announced an adjournment for lunch. Only a quarter of the candidates had been considered.

THE MEETING RECONVENED AFTER LUNCH, but Bob found it increasingly difficult to give it his whole attention. His supporters were willing to vote with him, but not to support him in other ways, so that unless and until he forced a vote to be taken, he appeared, in every case, to be fighting a lone fight. His opponents, on the other hand, were large in number, vocal, and seemed to have inexhaustible reserves of energy. They did not concede an inch of territory without a battle. His views were opposed at every stage, even by the chairman, who always objected to a request for a vote.

The meeting ended at 4.30 pm, and Bob crossed the dual carriageway and walked slowly up to his office on the top floor of the main polytechnic building. He felt tired and wondered what had been achieved. He had already acquired, among the staff, the reputation of being someone who enjoys prolonging meetings, and today's events would enhance this. In addition, although the proceedings of Examination Board meetings were supposed to be confidential, he knew that the students knew that he always led the attack on weak candidates with examination failures. Last year, there had appeared on notice boards a number of anonymously drawn cartoons featuring him in the role of executioner of students. His head of department wouldn't be pleased either. Last term Bob had received from him a "friendly note", typed on official polytechnic headed paper, enjoining him to "exhibit greater flexibility" in his work, and, since he had no way of telling what use was made of the carbon copies, didn't want another added to his record.

What made Bob especially angry with the Examination Board meeting was that he had put too much energy into the discussion about the first-year student called Evans, whom he liked and whom he knew had been genuinely ill and was certainly hard-working. His determination not to show bias in favour of Evans, however, had resulted in his being excessively severe to him. By the time the discussion had reached the students who were lazy, corrupt, or incompetent, his ammunition was spent and his troops, lacking leadership, were useless.

BOB GOT HOME TIRED as usual, but looking forward to the evening as Christine would be coming around to his flat for supper. Christine was a very dear friend, perhaps his only close friend, whom he had known almost as long as he had lived in Dunton. They saw each other several times a week.

Bob told her everything that happened to him at the polytechnic, and this usually helped him to see the events in their proper perspective. He had no secrets from her, and could feel completely relaxed in her company. She regarded herself as his girlfriend, but he shied away from such terminology; it implied too much of a long-term commitment, and. although he was unable to explain to her why, he was frightened of long-term commitment. The only subject he refused to discuss with her was marriage.

Christine was already at Bob's flat when he arrived. She had gone there straight from the school for handicapped children where she taught, and had started preparing a meal. It baffled Bob that he was happy for her to have a key to his flat, but wouldn't, despite her encouragement, consider getting married.

He was very pleased to see her, and, while washing the breakfast dishes and laying the table, told her about his last two days at the polytechnic. She had her own tales to tell of incompetent teachers and uncooperative parents, and he knew she told no-one else. She had recently applied for a promoted post at a school in Hamberbury, over a hundred miles away, and he wondered how he would manage if she was successful.

After supper they sat down together to read and to talk, and he told her that Eleanor would be coming to see him in two weeks' time. Christine put her book down and looked him in the eye.

"Why don't you get rid of that woman?" she said with uncharacteristic bluntness.

Bob was startled. Christine had never spoken to him like this before.

"Look, Christine," he said, "I know Eleanor irritates you.

She does me too. But she's an old friend and she wants to visit me."

"Am I only a new friend?" asked Christine brashly. "I've asked you to get rid of her. She makes me cross. You can't expect me to cook suppers for you if you're inviting Eleanor here."

Bob suddenly felt he was back in the polytechnic Board Room.

"I didn't invite her," he insisted quietly, "and I don't even like her. And, please note, I do not expect you to cook meals for me. I did not ask you to do so tonight, nor would I have complained if you had asked me to do it. And, even if I wanted to, which I don't, I can't prevent Eleanor from visiting Dunton because she's in Copenhagen this week and Cairo next week, and I don't know how to contact her."

"Right, that's it, then," said Christine, standing up and moving towards the front door of the flat.

"Hold on," said Bob, taken by surprise, "What do you mean: 'That's it'?"

Christine turned on him angrily. "You know perfectly well what I mean," she shouted, and went out of the flat, slamming the door. A moment later, he heard her drive away, her car roaring at maximum revs in first gear, and her car radio blaring at full volume.

Bob sank into an armchair. Examination Boards were bad enough, but an Examination Board meeting and a row with Christine on the same day was more than he could cope with, especially since he didn't understand what the row was about. ·To cap it all, he'd missed *The Archers* tonight, and was certainly in no mood to sit at his desk and write.

3

Bob got to his office early the next morning and, since he had no meetings to attend and the memos in his pigeon-hole were of only moderate urgency, decided to do something about his publications record. The trouble with his list of publications was that it had nothing on it. He was desperate to get some work published for several reasons. It was partly a matter of personal satisfaction. In one of his persistent daydreams, he referred his students to his own work in the polytechnic library and then smiled modestly and explained that his major book had been too expensive to be purchased on this year's library budget. He was also conscious that Christine had published several articles on her approach to the learning difficulties of children with cerebral palsy and that these had led to invitations to present papers at conferences. She had even been contacted by a publisher who wanted her to contribute to and edit a textbook of child development. In addition, her book of children's stories yielded a regular royalty income. While he shared her joy at this success, he was irritated that he had none of his own to celebrate with her.

He also wanted to publish to improve his standing in the polytechnic. His head of department had published three articles, but two of these were in the *Dunton Herald* and the most recent was seventeen years ago, so it would not be difficult to overtake him. If he could establish some credibility as a researcher, he might perhaps be able to get some of his administrative duties transferred to another lecturer.

The final reason for Bob's anxiety to see his name in print in an academic journal was that he hoped it might help him find another job. He had filled in without success many application forms for teaching posts in universities and polytechnics in the last two years, and he always disliked having to leave blank the section marked "Publications". His contribution to his grammar school magazine fifteen years earlier obviously did not count, and his quarter-page in *The Times Higher Education Supplement* last year (titled "The Mood of the Polytechnics") had become an embarrassment, and had nothing to do with his subject anyway.

He had two articles in hand, both of which had absorbed many hours of work and both of which, to his dismay, had already been rejected by several journals.

The longer of his two articles was particularly awkward to deal with. Each editor had sent a detailed referee's report, and this, in each case, explained the article's weaknesses and described suggestions for its improvement, but Bob found these barely comprehensible. This was because he did not fully understand his article either, but didn't dare admit this to anyone but Christine, who was not very helpful because she did not believe that anyone could write an article without being able to understand it. She had no such difficulties with her published work.

Bob had described to Christine many times that the article was based on work he had done during his previous job as a research assistant at Northleigh University. He had followed the instructions of his professor who had seemed, eventually, to be pleased with the outcome, but although Bob had frequently asked for an explanation of the statistical techniques he was applying, the professor had almost always been too busy to provide this. On the few occasions when he had tried to enlighten Bob, his helpfulness had quickly turned to exasperation when he found how little Bob knew about statistical method and how difficult he found it to think and speak in algebra.

Bob looked at the latest referee's report.

"The author has applied the Durbin-Watson test without assessing its validity and has not interpreted the results adequately. He/she has correctly identified that multicollinearity is a potential or actual problem, but has not taken appropriate action to deal with this. A fourth-difference equation might give interesting results, and deviations from the trend established might also be worth exploring."

That was only one of seven paragraphs, and Bob was lost already. He realised now that he should never have accepted the job at Northleigh, but it was too late to worry about that now. The important thing was to salvage something of the article.

Under his office desk Bob had three cardboard boxes full of computer-output paper covered with thousands, or perhaps even millions, of numbers. This was the fruit of two years' work at Northleigh, and his task was to make it not only edible but tasty. He had puzzled over this for hours and hours and hours over a four-year period, but still refused to concede defeat. This morning, he decided to postpone action until the latest Examination Board meeting and the row with Christine had become more distant memories.

Bob's second unpublished article had been much more interesting to write, although it had, as yet, been no more successful. It was a description of the latest round of controls announced by the Bank of England, with a discussion of their likely effects on the UK economy and their relationship to the banking reforms of 1971 and 1981. The article was original and, he felt, dealt with an issue of importance in a thorough way. To his great satisfaction, journal editors expressed their liking for it. He was bitterly disappointed, though, that they also found excuses for not publishing it. Bob laid three rejection letters in a row on his desk. The first said:

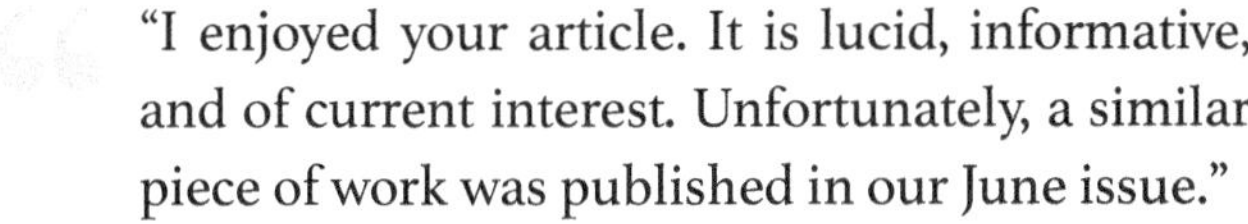

> "I enjoyed your article. It is lucid, informative, and of current interest. Unfortunately, a similar piece of work was published in our June issue."

The second letter said:

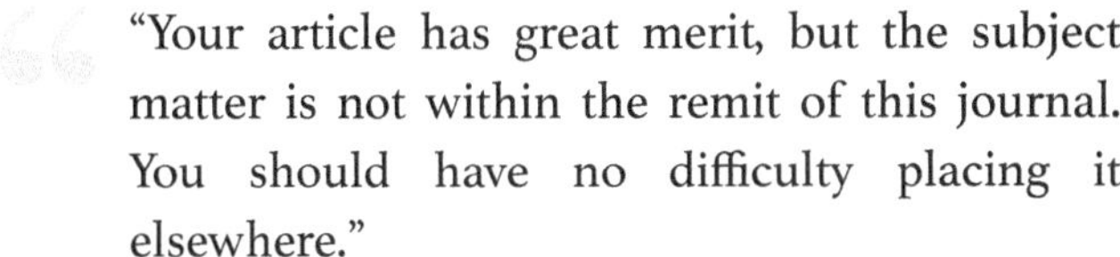

> "Your article has great merit, but the subject matter is not within the remit of this journal. You should have no difficulty placing it elsewhere."

Bob had replied to this one by asking for suggestions of suitable journals, but had not received any response.

The third letter was from an American publisher:

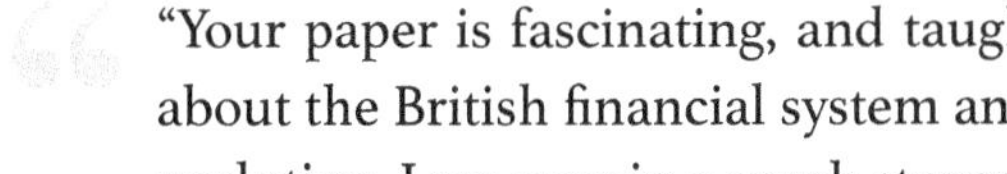

> "Your paper is fascinating, and taught me a lot about the British financial system and its recent evolution. I am now in a much stronger position

to understand books published in your country. My journal, however, deals with banking in the US context, so I cannot consider publishing your work."

Bob sighed. Each editor seemed to be playing by a different set of rules, and there seemed to be no prospect of winning.

There was a knock at his office door and, without waiting, in walked Martin Evans, who had failed his first-year examinations at the second attempt. He was looking flushed.

"I hope you're satisfied, now that I've failed again," he said.

"Of course I'm not satisfied," said Bob, "I wanted you to pass."

"No you didn't, you failed me."

"No," said Bob with emphasis, "That was the decision of the Examination Board as a whole, and the external examiners take a full part in the proceedings."

"That's not what I've heard. You wanted me out, didn't you?"

"No," said Bob, wondering why he had ever liked this student.

"Anyway, I've appealed, and you'll get egg on your face."

He went out, slamming the door.

Since Martin Evans' interruption had, for the moment, destroyed any possibility of tackling the publications problem, Bob walked along the corridor to the departmental secretary's office. When he first came to the polytechnic, before he met Christine, he used to confide in the secretary, but since then her workload had increased sharply, and she no longer had time to chat. Today, as usual, her typewriter was clattering at top speed, and there was a pile of uncompleted work at her elbow. He greeted her briefly.

In his pigeon-hole was a memo from the Registrar of the polytechnic, informing him that Martin Evans had appealed against a decision of the BA in Economics Examination Board and instructing him to appear before the Appeals Board later that week. There was the cryptic codicil: "Documentary evidence has been submitted." Bob wondered what that might mean.

LATER THAT DAY, there was an urgent knocking at Bob's office door. He opened it, without leaving his desk-chair, and was delighted to see the departmental secretary.

"Come in. Nice to see you," he said brightly.

"I've just had a telephone call from Mrs Lowson."

"Oh, not again," said Bob, slumping forward onto his desk in a mime of despair. Mrs Lowson telephoned him at the polytechnic for guidance from time to time. The first time it had happened he had tried, at her request, to explain on the telephone how to change a fuse, but this was beyond his teaching skills and led to exasperation of both parties. Such mistakes he tried to make only once, and his practice now was to ask the secretary to say he was busy.

"Just say that I'm ..." began Bob, but he was interrupted: "No, this time it's important. Your flat's been burgled."

Bob stood up immediately, banged his head on a coat-hook, and sat down again with a bump and a howl. The secretary tried hard not to laugh.

Bob gathered a few possessions, stuffed them into his briefcase and rushed out of the building. He ran across the dual carriageway to the car park and it was just luck that the lorry that swerved and the bus that braked did not collide. He drove home at a reckless speed.

Mrs Lowson was standing by his front door looking distraught. The door had been forced and hung open at a different angle from usual. Mrs Lowson started talking as soon as she saw Bob, but he held up his right hand for silence and interrupted, trying to appear more efficient than *he* felt: "Two questions, Mrs Lowson. One: has anything been stolen? Two: are the police still here?"

Mrs Lowson looked pained. "Police? What police? The police don't know about this."

"Why not?" said Bob, "Didn't you phone them?"

"Oh no," said Mrs Lowson, "I didn't think you would want the neighbours to see a police car outside your flat."

Bob pushed her aside and went into his flat to dial 999.

When he had finished, he saw Christine standing in the doorway. She was carrying two full supermarket bags.

"I've come to cook you a meal," she said.

"And supposing I don't want you to cook me a meal?" said Bob.

"Of course you do," said Christine, and went to make a start in the kitchen. Bob could see Mrs Lowson grinning at the spectacle. Christine came back from the kitchen. "If I do the breakfast dishes, will you feel redundant and angry?" she asked.

"No," said Bob, laughing and going with her into the kitchen. At least Christine was back, he thought.

Two police officers arrived within a few minutes. They made detailed notes and tut-tutted politely as Bob explained what he knew about the burglary. They could not give any assurance that the intruder would be caught. They did not stay long enough to sit down.

Eleanor telephoned just as Bob and Christine were

finishing the breakfast washing up. Christine pretended to be examining her toenails while Bob spoke on the telephone. He was trying to explain that perhaps a visit to Dunton was not the best idea, but there was a constant sound of frying and a simultaneous conversation in Danish to contend with, and the line went dead before he had got his point across.

"Thanks for trying," said Christine, as she returned to the kitchen. Bob followed but was ordered out. Christine said she was cooking a special meal to apologise for the row, and he was to wait in an armchair until called. Bob did as he was told but with bad grace he found difficult to conceal. He was hungry, and he was tired. His house had been burgled, and the police were not optimistic about finding the intruder. He had done an emergency repair to the front door but a professional was needed to do the job properly. Martin Evans had "documentary evidence" – what could that mean? And Christine, from the best of motives, of course, wouldn't let him eat. She wouldn't even let him into his own kitchen.

He knocked at the kitchen door. (Why should he have to knock at his own kitchen door?) The shouted reply was: "Don't come in."

He sat down and tried to ignore his rumbling stomach.

An hour later he knocked again and got the same response.

Thirty minutes after that, Christine emerged from the kitchen and asked if he had any candles.

"Candles?" asked Bob, amazed. "What do you want candles for?"

"To put on the table," said Christine.

"For goodness sake, Christine," said Bob, "I don't need candles. I just need food. You've kept me waiting two hours, and I'm hungry. Now."

Christine said nothing, but looked hurt. Bob sat down at

his place and started eating as soon as the plate was put in front of him. He had finished half the meal before Christine had hung up her apron and sat down. She was only just beginning to eat when he finished completely.

"That was good, Christine," said Bob. "I was very hungry."

Christine stared at him, furious. "You've ruined the meal by eating it too fast. You gobbled the food up without enjoying it. You've no table manners. I worked hard to produce this special meal, and you didn't even ask what it is. It's all wasted on you. You're hopeless."

Bob suddenly felt that Examination Board feeling again.

"Christine," he said patiently, "I've had a difficult day. I wanted to eat two hours ago. I didn't ask you to cook a special meal. I didn't ask you to cook a meal at all. You don't need to buy my friendship by cooking special meals. Don't you understand?"

"Yes," said Christine, moist-eyed," I understand." But Bob thought she didn't. She came and sat very close to him and put her arms around him. He knew there would be no point in sitting at his desk tonight.

4

At half past two the next day, Bob made his way, as instructed, to the polytechnic Board Room for the meeting of the Appeals Board. He sat down on one of the line of chairs in the corridor outside. He was surprised that he did not have to wait long. At 2.32 pm, only two minutes behind schedule, the Board members ended their half-hour private meeting and he was invited to join them.

On one side of the long table sat the four members of the Appeals Board, together with the Registrar of the polytechnic whose role was to take notes. There were two lay members of the Governing Body of the polytechnic, and two lecturers. In order to be fair, the latter were chosen so that their subject expertise was not relevant to the cases being considered. One taught biology and the other civil engineering. The chairman of the Board was a Conservative member of the County Council. The average age of the academic members of the Board was a little over 26 years. The average age of the lay members of the Board was almost 73 years.

The elderly chairman greeted Bob affably and invited him to be seated on the other side of the table. He started by expressing the appreciation of the Board that Bob had given up his time so willingly, especially at such a busy season for polytechnic lecturers. (I received a summons, thought Bob.) The chairman apologised for the short notice of the meeting, but explained that the imminence of the new term meant that a decision should be reached without any undue delay.

"Hear, hear. Hear, hear," said his lay colleague, who almost repeated the message for the sake of clarity, but the chairman silenced him with a glare.

The chairman asked Bob to summarise the basis of the Examination Board's decision concerning Martin Evans.

"Mr Evans," explained Bob, "failed his first-year examination in Economic Theory in June, was offered a resit examination, which he took in September, and failed this too. Both the marks were agreed by the external examiners. Last week, the Examination Board, with the agreement of the external examiners, decided that, since there were no mitigating circumstances, he should not be permitted to enter the second year of the course, but was offered the opportunity to repeat the first year of the course."

"Thank you," said the chairman, "that is a clear statement of the facts. Now, Mr Morgan, two documents have been submitted by Mr Evans and I would like you to read them and let us hear your comments."

He handed Bob two sheets of paper. The first had a printed heading – "The Surgery, St Georges-in-the-Wood, Duntonshire. Telephone St Georges-in-the-Wood 14". The telephone number had been crossed out and replaced with "Dunton 621414" in handwriting. The letter, in the same hand-writing, stated: "I certify that Martin Evans was unwell between 11th and 24th January". There followed an illegible signature. The letter was undated. Bob was not impressed.

The second letter, which had been inexpertly typed, ran:

"Dear Sir, I can assure you that Martin Evans is a very serious student, and I'm sure that his examination marks do not represent his real worth." This letter was signed by Martin Evans's father. Bob was even less impressed.

He was, however, now becoming confident of a successful outcome.

"Mr Morgan?" said the chairman.

"Let us take the medical certificate first," said Bob. "Mr Evans' illness in January was considered at the Examination Board meeting, but it was decided that it was not relevant. It was well before the examination."

The older lay member of the Board indicated his disagreement by shaking his head vigorously. "Illness can have long drawn out effects," he said, "and we should consider this."

"Yes," said Bob, "some illnesses can have such effects. But we are told nothing about the nature of the illness, and we are told that it ended on 24th January, more than seven months before the resit examination."

"I expect the illness lasted much longer than that, maybe several months. My brother-in-law is a doctor, you know, so I know about these things."

Bob had a strong desire to kick his opponent's shins, but overcame it.

"We can only consider the evidence before us," said Bob. "We cannot assume that the doctor is not telling the whole truth. In any case, if the illness was prolonged, as you suggest, it would have prevented the student from studying effectively. This is not acceptable grounds for condoning a failure mark. We should only take account of illness if it occurred during or just before the examination and inter-fered with the assessment process. We are concerned with the student's achievements, not with his intentions, so if, for any reason, he has not mastered the course material, we must fail him."

"Mr Morgan," said the chairman after a thoughtful pause, "I think it is my prerogative to rule on what we may or may not consider."

"Then please do so," said Bob.

"I … um … I agree entirely with your submission," said the chairman.

"Thank you," said Bob.

There was a silence. The meeting had lost its way, but fortunately the Registrar had a map. "There is a second document to be considered," he said.

"Ah yes," said the chairman. "Have you any comment on that, Mr Morgan?"

Bob looked again at the typewritten letter. "This letter must be regarded as irrelevant," he began, but the chairman raised his eyebrows and so Bob apologised and started again. "I regard this letter as irrelevant." The chairman smiled encouragingly, and Bob continued. "Because Mr Evans' level of diligence is not in dispute. Many of his lecturers described him, at the Examination Board meeting, as hardworking. Despite this hard work, however, he has failed on two occasions. In any case, his father is in no position to comment on the progress of his son's studies. A close relative cannot be regarded as an unbiased witness." The chairman raised his eyebrows, so Bob tried again. "A close relative is unlikely to be able to act as an unbiased witness." The chairman smiled. "In this particular case," continued Bob, "the student does not live at his parents' home during term, so his father is especially unlikely to know about his son's studies."

"The student's living arrangements are not the concern of this Board," said the chairman.

"Neither is this letter," said Bob.

The chairman scowled at him.

"Sorry," said Bob, "I withdraw that remark."

"I wish to make a ruling," said the chairman, "I rule that the letter from Martin Evans' father cannot be considered."

"Are you sure that's altogether wise?" said the older lay member. "After all, parents know their children. No-one knows my son better than I do, even though he's lived in Australia for twenty-four years."

"I have made a ruling," said the chairman.

"Oh, very well," said his colleague.

"Now," said the chairman, "there should be another of Mr Evans' teachers waiting outside to see us, so I shall ask Mr Morgan to withdraw."

The Registrar of the polytechnic coughed. "You might perhaps ask Mr Morgan if he has any final comments."

"Yes," said the chairman. "Mr Morgan, have you any final comments?"

"Yes," said Bob. "I notice that Mr Evans is not present at this meeting. Is that the usual practice?"

"He was invited to attend," said the chairman.

"Did he send an apology or explanation for his absence?" asked Bob.

"No," said the chairman.

"You may perhaps wish to consider this to be an indication of the student's attitude to the polytechnic," said Bob, deliberately being tentative, in order to avoid the chairman's raised eyebrows.

"Much as I sympathise with you," said the chairman, "I rule that submission to be not relevant to the matter before us."

"Hear, hear. Hear, hear," said his colleague.

After expressions of thanks were exchanged across the table, Bob left the room. Neither of the academic members of the Board had made a contribution to the discussion. In the corridor, one of Bob's opponents at the Examination Board meeting was waiting for his turn. Bob greeted him, and watched him enter the Board Room.

It would be two days before the decision of the Appeals Board reached him, but suddenly Bob found that he didn't really care what happened to Martin Evans.

WHEN BOB GOT BACK to his office, there was a note stuck to the door with sellotape. He pulled it off and, in doing so, removed a strip of gloss paint to reveal bare brown wood. There were many such strips of brown wood on his office door. The note said: "Please call at Police HQ and ask for Sergeant Johnston CID. This is urgent." He tried to guess what this was about but could not. He went along to the departmental office to seek clarification, but the secretary could only say that she had written down the telephone message exactly as it was dictated. She could see that he was worried, and added, "If they were going to arrest you, they would have come to the polytechnic instead of telephoning." This was obviously true, but didn't stop Bob wondering what he was supposed to have done. He considered ignoring the message, but decided that might create more problems than it solved.

AT THE POLICE STATION, Sergeant Johnston took Bob into a small room furnished with a table and three chairs. They both sat down.

"Now, sir," said Sergeant Johnston, "just a few routine questions."

"Yes," said Bob.

There was a long pause.

"I expect you know what this is about," said Sergeant Johnston.

"No," said Bob.

"That's what they all say," said Sergeant Johnston.

There was another long pause.

"Are you going to tell me what this is about?" asked Bob.

"Of course," said Sergeant Johnston.

There was a silence, but Bob was becoming less tolerant of silences.

"Am I under arrest?" asked Bob.

"Oh no," said Sergeant Johnston, "just helping the police with their enquiries."

"Am I free to go?" asked Bob.

"Certainly, but I think you'd be wise to answer my questions first."

There was a shorter pause.

"Can we make a start on your questions?" asked Bob, still baffled.

"That's a better attitude," said Sergeant Johnston. "Now, I understand that there was a burglary at your flat yesterday."

"Yes," said Bob, immediately relieved. This simple explanation had not entered his mind.

"I understand," said Sergeant Johnston, "that a new television was stolen."

"Yes," said Bob.

"And have you submitted a claim to your insurance company?"

"Yes," said Bob.

"Ah," said Sergeant Johnston, "that's interesting." Bob

couldn't see why, and was about to ask, but the sergeant was still talking. "When you telephoned us, you told us that approximately one hour had elapsed since the break-in, and you could give us no description of the intruder."

"That's right," said Bob. "My neighbour, Mrs Lowson, heard the noise and came to investigate, and the intruder ran off before she could see him."

"Ran off? With a television?"

"Well, walked off, perhaps. Or maybe he had a car."

"Why didn't Mrs Lowson phone us?"

"She thought I might not approve."

"And why is that?"

"That is impossible to explain," said Bob, smiling. "Mrs Lowson's behaviour constitutes one of the world's last great unsolved mysteries. Like why the Tower of Pisa doesn't fall."

"I see," said Sergeant Johnston, making notes but not amused. "I'll arrange to have a chat with Mrs Lowson."

"Do let me know how you get on," said Bob brightly.

"No," said Sergeant Johnston, still not smiling, "I shall not be submitting a report to you on my conversation with Mrs Lowson."

"Just a little joke," said Bob.

"I see," said Sergeant Johnston. "Now the other aspect of this case that concerns us is that yours were the only finger-prints on the door of your flat."

"Perhaps the intruder wore gloves," said Bob.

"That's what they all say," said Sergeant Johnston." Are you sure it wasn't you who removed the television in order to make a fraudulent insurance claim?"

"Of course not," shouted Bob, suddenly angry.

"That will be all, Mr Morgan," said Sergeant Johnston, opening the door of the interview room.

ON THE DOOR of Bob's office at the polytechnic, another note was held in place with sellotape. He pulled it off and removed another rectangle of paint. "Please collect a parcel from the departmental office" was the message.

He collected the parcel, and found that it contained a book with a note from the editor of one of the professional journals in his field, asking him to write a review. The secretary was, as usual, too busy to chat, but the parcel was enough to lift his spirits. He was invited to write book reviews about twice a year, and he felt that, although not equivalent to original publications in his own name, this was the next best thing. A request to review a book constituted some sort of recognition in the world outside Dunton Polytechnic, even if it only came from the editor of a low-prestige monthly periodical who had refused to publish both of his articles.

He had not arranged to see Christine that evening, so, after his meal (two fish fingers and a three-inch pyramid of peas), his post-meal nap, and *The Archers,* he sat down at his desk to write. Bob always found it difficult to start a piece of writing, but he had convinced himself that authors who were established and famous had the same problem. He unpacked the book. It had almost 800 pages, but he was not daunted. He knew that no book reviewer actually read the books under review. His usual policy was to start by making notes from the publisher's blurb on the dust-jacket; this indicated what the publisher thought the author had said. Then he made notes from the preface and the conclusion; this indicated what the author wanted to say. Then he would open the book at random half a dozen times to identify passages to quote. The final step was to weave his notes together into a piece of writing that was both informative and capable of holding the reader's attention. He regarded the ideal book review as thought-provoking but not unkind to the author, who may, as the editor of another journal, be considering publishing one of Bob's articles.

Bob's last book review had taken a month to write, but he decided that this one would be completed in a tenth of that time.

To get the flavour of the book, before starting on the publisher's description, Bob opened it in the middle, and was confronted by a double-page spread of algebra. He shuddered. He closed the book and opened it at a different page. This time only half the area of paper in front of him was covered with mathematical symbols. He felt no happier. This kind of book, he knew, was incomprehensible to him. It really belonged to an alien culture that was not accessible to him. He tried the foreword, but was not enlightened. He understood the meaning of the words, taken individually, but couldn't make much sense of the sentences, paragraphs, and pages. It was rather like wading along a fast-flowing river. He had the sensation of walking forward, but knew he was making no progress.

The answer, of course, was to take the bull by the horns. (At moments like this, the old sayings had real meaning!) He would not let lack of knowledge inhibit detailed commentary. Those who understood the book would be able to follow his broad generalisations, and those who didn't would presumably not be interested.

Bob made a start on writing the review. He referred to the subject matter of the book in only the most general terms but described it generously: "... detailed analysis ... clearly expressed ... relevant to issues of importance ... refers to the latest research results ... filling a gap in the range of specialised texts ... identifies and reconciles the views of the major schools of thought ... principally of interest to post-graduates and senior undergraduates." He wrote that: "... the author is to be congratulated on his scholarly work ... a masterly compilation of theory ... systematically assesses the flaws in opposing philosophies."

Two hours later, Bob got up from his desk. He had written a review to beat all other reviews. The following morning it was typed and posted. The response he received from the journal editor a week later was: "Thank you for such a perspicacious and well-balanced review."

5

───────

At the appointed hour on the appointed day, Bob ambled along the corridor from his office. He was carrying a cup of coffee to show that he understood that the meeting to which he was going was, as specified in the formal typewritten invitation from the head of department, an "informal gathering". He joined other lecturers, also holding cups of coffee and, in some cases, packets of biscuits, who were slowly making their way to the classroom where the meeting (or "informal gathering") was to be held. When they got near their destination, they could hear the sound of furniture being dragged across a floor. A glance around the doorpost revealed that Ken Park, the head of department, was, single-handedly, rearranging the chairs and tables from their traditional rows facing the blackboard to a rectangle reminiscent of the Board Room table. The lecturer who had been first to arrive put his forefinger to his lips and Bob and his colleagues nodded silently and retreated down the corridor a few yards to wait until furniture movement had ceased.

As they entered the room, they were greeted individually,

though not by name. The head of department was, by now, a little out of breath. "Hullo … Good morning … Nice to see you … Good of you to come … Come on in … It's good to see you … How are you … Glad you could make it …"

Gradually, the seats filled. Some people were late and the proceedings did not start promptly, but, since it was an "informal gathering", everyone pretended these things did not matter.

The head of department held up his hand for silence.

"May we make a start please? I think we …"

Someone interrupted: "Mr Park, may I ask …" but got no further.

"It's *Doctor* Park," said someone simultaneously with the head of department saying: "No, please, call me Ken. This is an informal gathering."

Bob looked around with a smile. It was a curious kind of informal gathering: typewritten invitation on headed paper, near-compulsory attendance, tables arranged in a rectangle, head of department in the chair …

"Before we begin, Ken," said the original interrupter of the chairman's opening remarks, "may I ask whether anyone will be taking minutes during this meeting?"

"No," said Ken Park, "no minutes will be taken. This is an informal gathering rather than a meeting, and I want discussion to be completely free and uninhibited."

"With respect, I beg to differ," was the reply. "You may recall that there were a number of disputes after last year's meeting about what had been decided. Your memory was different to everyone else's."

"There are several misunderstandings here," said the head of department. "First of all, this is not a meeting, and has no power to make decisions."

"In that case, I'm going," said his opponent. "I can't waste a day attending a meeting that isn't a meeting, and I'm not alone in thinking this." He stood up and strode out of the room, but no-one followed.

"Secondly," continued the chairman as if nothing had happened, "I want to know the mood of the staff of my department on a range of important issues, so I don't want anyone to be worried that hasty remarks will be used in evidence against them later."

"That is exactly the point," said Bob. "Some of us are frightened of being quoted or misquoted, and a written record might reduce the chance of errors."

He paused, and then went on: "Or abuse."

The chairman looked startled. "I hope you're not implying ..." he began.

"Oh no," said Bob sweetly.

With the matter of minutes unresolved and clearly in dispute, the chairman moved on to the first item on the agenda. Since it was an informal gathering and not a meeting, the agenda had not been distributed in advance.

"The first item," said the chairman, "and I have chosen this item to be first because I'm sure we will be able to dispose of it quickly, is the department's allocation of car parking spaces."

Immediately there was silence. This was an important item. Indeed, for several lecturers it was the only issue of departmental politics which aroused any interest.

"For the coming academic year," continued the chairman, "this department has been allocated seven spaces in the poly-technic car park. This allocation was done on a strict *pro rata* basis."

"What does that mean?" asked someone, but no-one else took any notice.

"At the last count," continued the chairman, "there were

eighteen members of the department who wish to use the car park."

"I make it nineteen," said one of his usual enemies.

"Can we leave the precise figure for the moment?" suggested the chairman.

"No, we can't, because the answer to a calculation depends on the numbers you use."

"But at this stage," insisted the chairman, "we're only discussing general principles."

"Why did you bring numbers into it then?"

The chairman was defeated. He sighed. "Evidently, I owe this informal gathering an apology." He tried to make a fresh start. "The problem before us is to devise a rota system so that everyone gets a fair share of the available spaces, which are strictly limited. I propose that the head of department has a space *ex officio*."

There was a mutter of disapproval. Perks for high earners were clearly out of favour, but Ken Park was undaunted. "Let us take your figure of nineteen," he said, "because it makes the sums easier.

"That's no reason for taking it," said someone, but everyone else pretended he hadn't.

"What I propose," said the chairman, "is that one space is reserved for me, which leaves the remaining six to be divided between eighteen members of staff, which means that each of you can use the car park one day in three."

There were more noises of disapproval, but its vocal form came from an unexpected quarter.

"What about me, and the others who don't own cars?" said one of the lecturers.

The chairman relaxed and smiled. This kind of opposition could be dealt with easily. "Those who do not own cars cannot expect to be allocated car park spaces." His smile was turning into a smirk.

"Oh yes we can. Those who use the polytechnic car park are saving the charge at the multi-storey. They are also receiving additional convenience. The right to use a car-park space is clearly a benefit with a money value, and should therefore be distributed evenly among lecturers. Those who don't own cars would therefore have two options: if capitalist, they might sell this right to the highest bidder and, if socialist, they could give it to the colleague in greatest need."

The chairman's smile had disappeared. He couldn't think of a flaw in the argument, but knew that there must be one. He wondered if such arguments were heard in departments other than Economics.

"Can I make a suggestion?" asked Bob. "This is essentially a simple problem, so it needs a simple solution. I suggest that spaces are not allocated to the head of department, or to any other individual, and neither is a rota drawn up. I suggest that it should be done on a first-come-first-served basis. Let those who arrive early have a space, and those who leave at lunch-time release a space for someone else."

Bob had expected his proposal to be uncontentious, but to his surprise, he found himself in a small minority. His opponents told him why.

"But I can't get to work early; I live twenty miles away."

"That's your choice," said Bob.

"I hate getting up early."

"That's your problem, not mine," said Bob.

"I take my children to school."

"Put them on the bus," said Bob.

"I go home for lunch and I want my space to be free for me when I return."

"Eat in the canteen like the rest of us," said Bob.

"You always get here early."

"You could too," said Bob.

"It's latecomers who have the greatest need for the convenience of the car park."

"Pass," said Bob.

After a lengthy discussion, during which were described fourteen separate models for the allocation of car parking spaces, no faction commanded a majority. The chairman announced that he would consider the matter very gravely and publish a decision in due course. No-one was satisfied.

He then moved on to the next item. More than an hour and a half had passed since the meeting started and two hours since it had been due to start. As soon as it was clear that there would be no further discussion on car-park spaces, several lecturers left, and many more followed during the next twenty minutes. When Bob left the room, some time later, there were only four people remaining, and the discussion had degenerated into a ritual. Winning or losing no longer mattered to the participants; the issue now was how they played the game.

Bob was in a state of anger and despair as he left the classroom. What he expected from his head of department was integrity and leadership, and he found neither. His colleagues were all such a grave disappointment to him, but perhaps they couldn't be blamed for reacting defensively to a stressful situation. Despite a complex and time-consuming structure of committees in the polytechnic, all important decisions were taken at the most senior levels. This was, however, frequently denied by Ken Park and the other heads of department.

Bob made a new resolution to find a new job, and decided once again that a publication or two might help. That pile of incomprehensible computer-output in his office would have to be tackled afresh.

AFTER LUNCH, Bab concentrated on a more immediate problem, and went to the garage where his car had been undergoing an MOT test. The garage proprietor shook his head sadly. "Couldn't pass it, sir, sorry. Defective steering. I could fix it for you though. Wouldn't cost you more than sixty pounds ... or ninety-five at the most."

Bob shook his head, paid the test fee and got into his car. It pitched and swayed as he drove out of the garage and he wondered what the scrap-iron and deep pools of oily water that he was driving over and through were doing to the car.

He drove across Dunton to the garage whose owner he trusted and showed him the MOT failure certificate.

The mechanic drew in his breath sharply. "Defective steering. Ooh yes, could be a big job. That'll be play in the king-pins, probably. I could do it for you tomorrow. Forty pounds."

Bob agreed, and took a bus back to the polytechnic.

ON HIS OFFICE door a piece of sellotape held a small envelope in place. It bore his name and the printed words: "OVER-SEAS TELEGRAM".

Puzzled, he tore it off and opened it. The door was beginning to look like a dalmatian. The telegram read: "ROBERT MORGAN DUNTON POLYTECH DUNTON GB REGRET VISIT DUNTON NOT POSSIBLE STOP NOW IN BERLIN ELEANOR".

Bob sighed with relief, and rushed to a telephone to tell Christine the good news.

He went home feeling simultaneously elated and irritated at the way the day had been spent. The "informal gathering" had not merely achieved nothing, it had exacerbated existing tensions in the Department of Economics. On the other hand, the news about the car was good, because he was expecting far worse. And the contents of Eleanor's telegram were a cause for celebration.

As he opened the door of his flat, Bob thought about the reasons for his good spirits. He felt that he must be in a very sorry state if the absence of bad news became a cause for celebration.

Later that evening Christine called at his flat. He had already eaten, and his mouth dropped open when he saw her bulging supermarket bag.

"Don't worry," she said, "it's not another special meal. It's some clothes I want to wash. There's no hot water in my flat tonight."

Bob made her a cup of tea to drink while doing her washing, which didn't take long. He took the wet clothes out to the washing line and started to hang them up to dry. Before he had finished, Mrs Lowson joined him.

"And what are you doing, young man?" she asked with a certain aggression.

"I'm hanging up Christine's underwear," replied Bob.

"I can see exactly what you're doing," said Mrs Lowson, "I don't need to be told."

"Then why ask?"

Mrs Lowson glowered at him. "Do you think it is right,"

she said, "for a single man to be publicly handling his young lady's smalls?"

"Yes," said Bob, and almost started laughing at the use of the word 'smalls'. Christine's were, certainly, exceptionally small. Quite a contrast to Mrs Lowson's, which he saw frequently on the line.

Mrs Lowson was clearly aroused by Bob's suppressed laughter. "I don't like your attitude," she said, and stormed off back to her flat.

"And I don't like yours," shouted Bob after her. He was feeling better than he had all day.

6

During the weekend, Bob tried, without success, to forget about the polytechnic. He saw quite a lot of Christine but resented it when she said that Saturday afternoon and evening were for her writing. She had almost finished another article, this time on "The Integration of Children with Osteogenesis Imperfecta into Mainstream Schools". And, he thought with some bitterness, she'd have no trouble finding a publisher. It didn't seem fair that she could be so relaxed and organised about her writing. It seemed too grand to call it literary activity if it received success so easily. Of course, he suppressed such views when in her company, and he knew that she always tried to be supportive about his writing. Sometimes he felt awkward about being so difficult to support.

On Saturday afternoon, after doing his weekly supermarket shopping (and Christine's, since she was writing), Bob went to collect his car. The owner of the garage presented him with a bill for £5.29. With any other garage he would have paid and driven away, but he liked this man and depended on him, so he queried the amount.

"I was expecting it to be forty pounds," said Bob.

"Forty pounds? For this little job? Don't be ridiculous!"

Bob hesitated, and then had another go.

"I thought there was play in the king-pins."

"Play in the king-pins? No, no, NO, no. Not at all. Not at all. No play in those king-pins."

"What was the problem then?"

"Just a bit of lift in the bushes."

"Is that all?" said Bob, pretending to understand.

"Yes, no trouble at all. Just a quick job."

Bob paid and drove home. He felt increasingly incompetent. If the garage man talked in this casual way about king-pins and bushes, to say nothing of the distinction between play and lift, then perhaps he really ought to understand at least part of what was said. Christine had the same effect on him when she talked about dyspraxia, posttraumatic hydrocephalus, and congenital syndactaly. He wrote a mental memo to himself: "Get educated".

When he got home, Mrs Lowson was waiting anxiously on his doorstep. He was not pleased to see her, and decided to take a hard line if necessary. He wasn't sure if he had won yesterday's confrontation.

He need not have worried. Mrs Lowson wanted to apologise.

"I don't know what came over me, getting so cross with you. And you being so helpful to young Christine when she's so tired after all that work with those poor crippled children. Anyway, here's another jar of my chutney to show I'm sorry."

Bob took the chutney, thanked Mrs Lowson, and shut the front door quickly before she could embark on a new topic. Checking that he could not be seen from the window, he placed the chutney in the kitchen cupboard with all the rest.

LATER THAT AFTERNOON there was a phone call from the Head Caretaker at the polytechnic.

"I've got an overseas telegram here addressed to you. Shall I keep it till Monday, or would you like me to open it and read it over the telephone?"

Bob asked him to read it to him immediately. The telegram said: "ROBERT MORGAN DUNTON POLY-TECHNIC DUNTON GB TRANSFERRED EDINBURGH NEXT WEEK STOP DUNTON VISIT BACK ON WHOOPEE ELEANOR".

Bob sat down. He suddenly had no desire to make whoopee with anyone.

HE CALLED ON CHRISTINE, as promised, at 9.30 pm. She was looking weary but was in very good spirits. She told him at great length about her article and he tried very hard to take an interest. It was difficult to follow something so complex, and several times he found that his concentration had wandered. And still she went on, telling him about the impor-tance of the ideas she was writing about.

He told her about the car and she tried to appear inter-ested. He then told her about Eleanor's second telegram, and she immediately sat upright and glared at him.

"All right, you can invite her. See if I care."

"Look," said Bob in desperation, "I didn't invite her." But Christine had locked herself in the bathroom, and could be heard singing loudly while she washed her hair. Bob shouted his Good Night and let himself out of her flat.

MONDAY MORNING WAS the start of the new term, and the polytechnic was alive with people and noise. A row of three large blackboards in the entrance hall of the main polytechnic building listed the number of the Enrolment Room for each year of each course. This was not very helpful to first-year students, almost all of whom were not familiar with the layout of the polytechnic buildings (inaccurately called a Campus in the pamphlets sent to secondary schools). Most of the buildings were within a mile of each other, but some were separated from the rest by an urban motorway. In attempting to cross this, pedestrians risked their lives and broke the law, but were not always deterred. Only well-established Duntonians could find the subway whose entrance was carefully concealed and misleadingly signposted. One of the polytechnic annexes was three miles away, but students on most courses completed their polytechnic careers without discovering this.

Bob entered the main polytechnic building, and stood and watched the crowd in the entrance hall. Second-year and third-year students ignored baffled new students who were asking each other which way to go and receiving no information. One unhappy female looked close to tears: "I didn't know it was going to be like this," she said again and again to no-one in particular. As Bob stood there, more and more students arrived and added to the crush, but very few made their way out to the Enrolment Rooms, which they did not know how to find.

Bob climbed the stairs to his office and collected his Enrolment Pack. This was a folder containing details of the new first-year students offered places on the BA in Economics course, a supply of Enrolment Forms for them to complete (in triplicate), duplicated timetables and booklists, and invitations from the Principal to attend the Induction Day.

Bob made his way, with his Enrolment Pack, down to the ground floor, through the crush at the entrance, and under the motorway to the Mary Street annexe. This was a building never shown to important visitors. It had originally been a textile mill, but for various periods of time parts of it had also functioned as a dance hall, carpet warehouse, car showroom, and chapel. The external facade had not been altered and still bore the arms of the original owner, but the interior had been changed so many times that the textile workers would have been unable to recognise it. Alterations to the building had been done cheaply and without care. Maintenance had been neglected and was now ruled out because at some time within the next five (or perhaps ten) years the building was to be demolished.

Among students the Mary Street annexe was known as The Slum, which was not inappropriate. Some of the windows wouldn't open and some wouldn't close. Rooms overlooking the motorway were intolerable because of traffic noise, and rooms overlooking the municipal swimming pool smelt of chlorine and disinfectant. The floors were uneven and the partitions were not sound-proof. Mould was widespread. Paint flaked off ceilings. In the winter students wore coats and scarves to lectures because the heating was inadequate. In the summer, because of the damp walls, it was not much better.

Bob's Enrolment Room was empty, so he laid out the various documents in neat piles and waited. After a while first-year students began to arrive. None had come by the shortest route. Those that had not reached the right destination were sent on their way with fresh instructions.

Provided their names were on the list in front of him, Bob

gave each student one copy of each of the documents in his Enrolment Pack. Such students then sat down at desks and filled in the Enrolment Form, on which they entered the same information as had already been supplied by them on the Application Form.

Students arrived singly and in groups for most of the morning. When their forms had been completed, Bob added his signature in the space marked Enrolling Officer. The students were then directed to deliver the completed, signed, and countersigned forms to the appropriate Registration Room for polytechnic identity cards to be issued. Production of such a card entitled the holder to claim a grant cheque and a locker key (not theft-proof) from yet another room.

Bob also had to deal with a trickle of students whose names were not on his list but who thought, often passionately, that they should be. He referred them to the Registry if they had already submitted an Application Form and to the Admissions Office if they had not, for there were still vacant places on the course.

This process continued, with varying degrees of intensity, all day. No academic activity took place at Dunton Polytechnic on Enrolment Day. The most used facilities were the coin-operated drinks machines. New students were already discovering which foreign coins could be exchanged for hot coffee. Second-year students were selling their least-used textbooks to new arrivals at a premium on the grounds that they were vital and out of print. Spotty males were watching females and being ignored. In the midst of all this, some students were very alone.

AFTER LUNCH BOB returned to his Enrolment Room to receive the stragglers. When he got there, he found six students waiting for him, including, to his surprise, Martin Evans. He hadn't bothered to find out whether Martin Evans' appeal had been successful and hoped that this would become clear quickly. It did.

"Hullo, Mr Bloody Morgan," said Martin Evans, when he saw Bob approaching.

"Good afternoon," said Bob.

"You've won, then."

"What does that mean?"

"You've succeeded in getting me off the course."

"That's not correct. It was the decision of the Examination Board and the Appeals Board. I had one vote at the Examination Board and none at the Appeals Board."

"That's your story."

"Yes, it is. I'm sorry about the decision, but you are being allowed to have another go."

"We'll see about that. You'd better start buying the *Dunton Herald*; this kind of victimisation is the sort of stuff journalists enjoy."

"Just get out, Mr Evans," shouted Bob. But he had already gone.

The five new students had watched this in silence. Clearly polytechnic life was not as uninteresting as they had thought.

AT THE END of the afternoon Bob returned to the main polytechnic building. He took the remains of the Enrolment Pack to the Registry. As usual, a substantial minority of the students who had been offered places had not enrolled. Even though more places had been offered than were available, this still left a shortfall, and, as the lecturer responsible for interviewing prospective students during the summer, he knew that he would be blamed. As an interviewer, he was supposed to market the polytechnic, and he always did his best to comply, but found it difficult to sound enthusiastic about an institution from which he was trying to escape. At least he would be able to say, when challenged, that he had not refused admission to anyone, however unimpressive. He did, however, confidently forecast a high failure rate this year, and was apprehensive about the attacks that would be directed at him in June; he knew that he would be blamed for accepting weak or uncommitted students.

From the Registry, Bob made his way up to his office. On the door was a note. He was getting a bit tired of notes on his door. This one said: "Please see me urgently". There was no signature, but he recognised the handwriting of Ken Park.

Dr Park's door was open, but Bob knocked anyway, and his head of department looked up from his copy of *The Times Higher Education Supplement*, which was open at a page of job advertisements.

"Come in, Bob. Come in," said Dr Park. "How did things go today?"

Bob knew that this was an enquiry about student numbers.

"Well," he said, and hesitated, "most of the students turned up, and I expect there'll be more during the week."

"Exactly how many enrolled?"

"Eighteen."

"What! We've thirty places! What is the Principal going to say? What are you doing about it?"

"There's nothing I can do."

"No, I suppose not." Dr Park subsided, and Bob relaxed.

"What are the numbers like on other courses?" asked Bob, playing the game by the rules.

"It's not absolutely clear yet, but the latest information I have is that things are not as bad as some people had feared."

This meaningless statement sounded to Bob like wartime propaganda intended to prepare the civilian population for news of heavy casualties on the Italian front.

"When will we know the exact position?" asked Bob, hoping that he sounded like an officer.

"Hard to say. Could be a week before things settle down. And a month before all the late enrolments have been counted."

There was a thoughtful pause.

"The main thing," continued Dr Park, "is that I've got to have a good explanation ready for the Principal. Can I ask you to think about this and jot down a few ideas for me by tomorrow morning? Shouldn't take you long; remember that the Principal doesn't understand economics – so it shouldn't be hard to baffle him. It must sound impressive, though."

"I'll do what I can," said Bob resignedly.

"I'd be very grateful," said Dr Park, and evidently meant it.

THAT EVENING, after *The Archers*, Bob sat at his desk and tried to think of some ideas for his head of department to say to the Principal. He knew that he was intended for literary activity on a higher plane than this, but it seemed to be impossible to convince anyone else.

7

———

On his way to the polytechnic the next morning, Bob stopped, as usual, to buy a copy of *The Guardian*. As it was a Tuesday this purchase was of special importance; each week the Tuesday issue contained several pages of academic job advertisements. All of the lecturers in his department bought *The Guardian* on Tuesdays, even those who usually read the *Daily Express*, because the one aim that they all had in common was the desire to find employment somewhere else. In their different ways, they were all weary of the overcrowded conditions, the long hours, and Ken Park's management style.

With his newspaper in his briefcase, Bob made his way to the polytechnic. Having collected his mail from his pigeon-hole at the main entrance, he went up to his office. Several of the letters he discarded without opening; a lot of advertising was sent to every lecturer on the staff of the polytechnic (and to some of those who had left many years earlier). Some of the internal mail he put on one side to deal with later; this included invitations to committee meetings which he hoped would clash with teaching commitments. Other internal mail went, after a cursory glance, into the waste-paper bin. There was nothing from either of the journal editors to whom he had sent his articles. After four minutes, he had dealt with seventeen items of mail; none were of importance, none required immediate action, and his bin was already half full of screwed-up paper.

Since his first class was not until ten o'clock, Bob opened his newspaper at the appointments advertisements and spread it out on his desk. He ran his fingers down the columns of small print. There were several pages to look at, each with nine columns. At the end of the first page he had not found a single vacancy for a lecturer in economics. Zoology, history, chemistry, classics, French, computing, physics, music, civil engineering, biochemistry, law, geology, theology, and every other subject under the sun was mentioned, but not economics. He turned the page, and, to his delight, saw the word "economics" at the top of the first column. Then he saw that the vacancy was at Cambridge, and moved his finger on down the column; there was no point in a lecturer at Dunton Polytechnic applying for a job at Cambridge.

Two pages further on, Bob reached the advertisement for a lecturer in economics at Blumington Polytechnic. He ringed it with his red biro, and resolved to write for details and an application form that evening. He went on looking, examining every advertisement in the Education section. There were no others in his subject. Still, he thought, one is better than none, so this week is better than most. He tried not to think of all the other economics graduates looking at the same pages of *The Guardian* that morning.

Today's important task completed, he started to prepare some lectures. He was well into this work when there was a knock at his office door. It was the head of the Department of Business Studies.

"I would have phoned," he said, but of course you haven't got a phone."

"No," said Bob.

"Gosh, this office is pokey, isn't it?"

"Yes," said Bob.

"I hadn't realised how lucky my staff are. It's the first time I've been up here to Economics."

"Yes," said Bob.

"But I'm glad I came; it's good to keep in touch, what?"

"Yes," said Bob.

"You seem to be working very hard. New term in full swing, eh?"

"Yes," said Bob, wondering when his unwanted guest would come to the point.

"To come to the point of this visit," said the head of the Department of Business Studies, "I'm sure you'll be interested, and indeed pleased, to know that I've heard from Jacksbridge Polytechnic. They want a reference on you, so you'll probably get an interview in due course. Jacksbridge is a miserable place, of course, but a job at the polytechnic there is bound to be better than working at this dump." He put his finger to his lips and added, "That comment was strictly off the record."

"Of course," said Bob.

"Anyway, I've got your *curriculum vitae* so I've got plenty of background information. Don't worry, I'll write you a good reference. I know how you feel; I'm keen to get out of this place too."

"I'm very grateful for your support and help," said Bob.

"That's OK. Pleased to help. By the way, I spoke to Ken Park on the way up here. He seemed quite surprised that you've applied to Jacksbridge. Didn't you quote him as a referee?"

"No," said Bob.

"Why not?"

"Because, well ... because I decided not to," said Bob, knowing it sounded weak.

"He is your head of department."

"Yes," said Bob, "but I feel he doesn't know me very well."

"On the contrary, I would say, from his remarks this morning, that he knows you extremely well."

"Yes, well, thank you anyway," said Bob, who was holding his door open to encourage his uninvited visitor to leave. He was trying to work out what that last remark meant. He was also irritated that some senior people didn't understand the meaning of confidentiality. Did he really have to explain it in detail?

LATER THAT DAY, Ken Park greeted Bob in a crowded corridor. People were moving in both directions, and the traffic jam was exacerbated by the queue at the coffee machine. This was hardly the place for a discussion of personal matters, but Dr Park was unaware of this.

"Heard you've been short-listed for a job at Jacksbridge Poly," he said in a loud voice.

"Yes," said Bob, aware that some of his students were taking more interest in him than usual.

"What makes you want to go there?"

"Well," said Bob, and hesitated, aware of his audience, "it would be a change."

"It certainly would," said Dr Park, and guffawed.

BOB ENTERED the main lecture theatre. With the exception of the first row, almost all the seats were taken. There was a buzz of conversation.

He stood behind the table at the front of the room and waited. At first no-one noticed he was there, and then suddenly students started shushing each other, and after a minute or two there was silence. He began his lecture to the new first-year students. It was a relaxed, polished, performance, and the students tried to write it all down.

In the middle of this successful professionalism, Bob recalled his very first lecture at Dunton Polytechnic. He had had no teaching experience, no teaching qualification, and no experience of public speaking before being appointed. Determined to make a good impression, he had prepared his first lecture in great detail, and had written out the final revision in long-hand. He had practised reading this in front of the bathroom mirror and had found that it took fifty-five minutes, which was clearly ideal, since it would leave time for a few questions before the end of the one-hour lecture period. He had entered the lecture room with confidence.

The confidence had soon vanished, however, when it had become clear that the students had been determined not to stop talking in response to his shouts for silence. Indeed, he remembered with acute embarrassment how, with each shout from him, the volume of students' conversations had increased. When eventually near-silence had been achieved, Bob had found that his lecture was impossible to read since his hands were shaking violently and his eyes were unable to focus on a moving target. He had finally made a start by putting his script on the table. This at least had kept it still, but his handwriting was small so he had had to bend over to read it. In this curious posture, he had read his lecture, but only the first three rows of students had been able to hear it.

After twenty minutes, he had reached the end of the lecture, and he had forgotten to invite questions. In his hurry to leave with an attempt at dignity, he had used the Emergency Exit, which, to his great surprise, had taken him straight out onto the pavement. The door had slammed shut behind him, and he had had to use the usual route to re-enter the lecture theatre, still full of the same students, to retrieve his briefcase.

The following week only four students out of eighty had attended his first-year lecture. Bob had felt that protest deeply.

Bob put these humiliating memories out of his mind, and concentrated on this morning's lecture. At the end of the hour he felt tired but exhilarated. This was the kind of work he liked doing.

WHEN HE GOT home that evening, there was a letter for him behind the front door. It was from Jacksbridge Polytechnic inviting him to attend an interview. He was delighted. Although he applied for almost every vacancy in his subject area, he had had only one interview in the last year.

He told Christine as soon as she arrived at his flat that evening. He told her that he was fairly confident, or even *very* confident, of getting this job, which was, after all, at a low-prestige polytechnic in a run-down city, so there shouldn't be many other applicants.

"Don't count your chickens too soon," said Christine, always the wise one, "and are you sure you want to go that far from Dunton?"

"I'd miss you," said Bob with great feeling. On the way home, he had been toying with the idea of asking her to marry him, but wasn't sure if this was the right moment. He didn't want her to feel she was being asked for the wrong reasons. On the other hand, the strong desire to be with her often was surely the best reason. He was also conscious that he had refused to discuss the issue many times, and now felt awkward about raising it. As so often happened, help came from Christine, but on this occasion he neither sought it nor expected it.

"If you get the job in Jacksbridge, would you be cross if I looked for a job there too?" asked Christine tentatively.

Bob was overjoyed. "Cross? Cross? Why should I be cross? Nothing would make me happier. But I didn't like to ask."

"Look," said Christine, pointing an index-finger at him in mock anger, "haven't I always said that if you've got something important to say, you should say it?"

She gave him a big affectionate hug.

"Christine," he said, when she had released him and he was able to breathe again, "I've got something else important to say."

"Go ahead," said Christine with a smile.

"Will you marry me?" he asked, suddenly feeling it sounded hackneyed.

He got another high-compression hug, and then she said, "I'll think about it. It is a very big decision. But I will definitely look for a job in the Jacksbridge area if you're successful at your interview."

Bob wanted to jump up and down and run out into the street to tell everyone. Even though she hadn't agreed to marry him, she certainly hadn't turned him down. And she had suggested, without any prompting from him, that she would move to a new town to be with him. He kept asking himself why he had always shied away from talking and, most of the time, even thinking about this kind of thing. Oh,

Callooh! Callay! O frabjous day! Lewis Carroll certainly had a way with words.

LATER THAT EVENING he tried to compose some notes for Ken Park to use when under attack by the Principal because of the low number of students in his department. It took Bob an hour to think of five points. He wrote:

"To: K. Park

From: R. Morgan

Possible Explanations for Low Enrolment on BA in Economics

1. Reduced birth-rate 18 years ago

2. Urban decay gives Dunton a bad name

3. Performance of government gives Economics a bad name

4. Graduate unemployment encourages students to choose courses related to specific professions (e.g. accountancy)

5. Etc

I hope this is helpful.

Robert Morgan."

He wasn't happy about any of these points, especially the fifth, but it was the best he could do.

The next morning, he left the note for his head of department.

IT WAS several days before he was, once again, accosted by Dr Park in a busy corridor.

"Got your note, Bob. Thanks. I've passed it to the Principal. Not sure what he'll make of it, but I'll let you know."

Bob was alarmed. "That note was for you, not for him. If I was writing to the Principal I'd have written much more formally, and I'd have said different things."

"Oh yes, and what would you have said?"

"Well, different things. I ... well I'm not sure if any of the reasons I gave are really explanations of why the trend is different for the BA in Economics compared to other courses."

"Why did you send the note to me then?"

"Because ... well ... you asked for a note. And it was better to say something than to say nothing."

"I see. But if you had nothing to say, it would perhaps have been better to say that you had nothing to say."

"Yes," said Bob, aware of the crowd of students listening with great interest.

"I shall remember this incident," said Dr Park.

"So shall I," whispered Bob after he had gone.

LATER THAT DAY, during her tea-break, Bob told the departmental secretary about his conversation in the corridor. She smiled. "You've no reason to be concerned," she said. "He asked me to type your notes into a memo from him to the Principal, who won't know that you had anything to do with it. If anyone looks silly, it'll be Ken, not you."

Bob walked down the stairs with a spring in his step that he hadn't felt since the first telegram from Eleanor.

8

———

His interview at Jacksbridge Polytechnic was a preoccupation of Bob's during the next three weeks. Using the appropriate form (Dunton Polytechnic provided a form for every purpose), he applied for, and was granted, permission to be absent from his duties on the day of the interview. He wondered if such permission had ever been refused, but there was no means of finding out.

Christine became coy about the subject of marriage. She continued to see Bob often but wouldn't discuss the issue. She insisted that she was thinking, and that this needed time.

Eleanor's visit had strengthened this mood of Christine's. Bob had found it a trial because Eleanor had insisted on telling at great length and in very great detail things that were of no interest to him. The layout of Amsterdam airport buildings, and the absurdities thereof, did not hold his attention. He couldn't remember most of the other topics that were so close to her heart. He had invited Christine to join Eleanor and himself for dinner on the Saturday night, and she was clearly aware of his impatience. He was relieved when Eleanor left the next day. He hoped it would be a long time before her next visit to Dunton, but it was evident that she had had a good time and thought that Bob had too.

Bob was very pleased when Christine wrote to the Jacksbridge education authority to enquire about vacancies for teachers of handicapped children. He proof-read her *curriculum vitae* and felt envious at her list of publications. He reminded himself, though, that his two articles, while experiencing a difficult birth, were nevertheless on the verge of being born.

THE EVENING BEFORE THE INTERVIEW, Bob set off for Jacksbridge.

He had driven no more than thirty miles when the radiator of his car overheated, and he braked sharply as he drove into a blinding cloud of steam. He brought the car to a halt on the grass verge and opened the bonnet. When the steam had cleared, the nature of the problem became obvious; the fan-belt had snapped. Cursing himself for not checking its condition before leaving Dunton, since a new MOT certificate is useless if the car won't go, he started to walk along the road to find a telephone. It was dark, the grass verge was neither level nor dry, and the cars moving past his shoulder at seventy miles an hour did not respond to his waves. After about an hour he reached a telephone kiosk and dialled the AA number. His name, address, and membership number were requested, followed by the registration number, make, and location of his car. The AA clerk assured Bob that help would be sent as soon as possible.

"Would you ask the mechanic to bring a fan-belt for an Allegro?" asked Bob.

"The mechanic will decide what is needed," was the

abrupt reply. Bob felt as though he was being reprimanded for forging a doctor's signature on a prescription for dangerous drugs.

He trudged back through the dark, occasionally stumbling on the wet muddy grass. It seemed further this time, but he was greatly cheered by the sight of a yellow AA van waiting for him beside his car. The mechanic was a round-faced cheerful man, who reminded Bob of Benny Hill playing the part of a round-faced cheerful AA mechanic.

Within five minutes, the car was ready to go, and Bob set off once again for Jacksbridge. He tried to work out whether the broken fan-belt should be regarded as a good omen for the interview.

His hotel was undistinguished, but Bob woke the next morning feeling refreshed and ready for the fray. After breakfast he walked to the polytechnic and, since he was a little early for his appointment, strolled in a park nearby to gather his thoughts and rehearse answers to likely questions. It was a small park and he noticed several other young men wearing formal suits also strolling around looking thoughtful. He approached one and asked, "Interview candidate for the economics job at the polytechnic?" His guess was right, and overheard by all the other thoughtful strollers, so the five short-listed candidates were able to compare their proposed tactics and approach the polytechnic buildings as a group.

They had been asked to report at 10.30 am to the secretary of the Department of Economics, Sociology, and Politics. This department was situated in a late-Victorian terraced house. For reasons that were not explained, the departmental secretary worked on the first floor. Her role was to direct the candidates to the head of department's room on the ground floor.

The head of department had been watching through his net curtains and had seen the five candidates arrive. He had heard them climb the stairs to the first floor and then come down again. Creaking wooden stairs reveal all to the practised ear. He was therefore sitting at his desk holding a pen with unfinished lecture notes in front of him, ready to greet his guests, when Bob knocked.

He opened his door and invited them in. He asked for each candidate's name, and promised not to get them mixed up. He pointed out that his office did not have enough chairs for all of them and that therefore he was asking none of them to sit down. He explained that the first activity of the day would be informal coffee with some of the staff of the department. This was to be held in a classroom on the first floor, so the five candidates were taken upstairs again.

Most of the staff of the department were in the classroom when the head of department arrived with the five interviewees. He called for silence, and then introduced the five: "I want you to welcome our visitors ... Dr Adamson, Or Burlew, Dr Fellowes, Dr Khan, and Mr Morgan ... who are to be interviewed this afternoon for the post of Lecturer in Economics." Bob started; he hoped his lack of a doctorate wasn't going to reduce his chances. "Now," continued the head of department, "I propose to see each of the candidates in turn in my office while the rest are having some coffee with members of the department. At 12 o'clock, I shall take our guests to the Tower Building for lunch with the interview panel. Formal interviews will begin at 2 o'clock. Any questions?" No-one moved, so he continued. "Right, can I see the candidates in alphabetical order?"

Dr Adamson followed him downstairs. It was the fourth time in ten minutes that he had made this journey.

Bob found the next hour extremely valuable. He chatted to each of the Jacksbridge lecturers in turn and was amazed how disloyal they were to their polytechnic in the presence of outsiders. They all freely admitted that they were looking for new jobs, and several asked him about conditions at Dunton Polytechnic. They all explained that the head of department, though well-meaning, was unable to do his job effectively.

When asked if he was popular, one lecturer said in a loud voice, "I expect some people think very highly of him, but I've never met any of them", and everyone laughed. Bob began to wonder if working at Jacksbridge was too high a price to pay to leave Dunton.

By the time his turn came to talk to the head of department, Bob had plenty of questions to ask and, furthermore, his conversations with junior staff had revealed the answers in advance. He duly asked his questions, and noted that he received misleading half-truths in reply. Even Ken Park could do better than this.

Lunch was formal, but enjoyable. Bob found the other candidates very likeable. They compared their experiences and it was encouraging to find that conditions at Dunton Polytechnic were not unique. The single candidate whose present post was at a university learned a lot about conditions in the other sector of higher education in his own country. The members of the interview board tried to participate in the conversation too.

After lunch, the candidates were shown into a staff common room which was to be used as a waiting room. They were told that they would be summoned, in alphabetical order, at half-hour intervals. Bob's turn was to be at 4 pm.

Rather than wait for two hours doing nothing much, Bob went for a walk around the city centre. He sent a postcard to Christine and then wondered how else to fill in the time. It was raining, so he went into the polytechnic library. He found the bound journals section, and quickly discovered that all Christine's articles were there. He was mostly pleased, but also a little envious. At 3.45 pm, after continuing to browse long after the mood had passed, he returned to the staff common room to await his turn for interview. He hoped that the fourth candidate's interview might have ended and that he would be able to get some advance warning of tricky questions.

To his surprise, not only had the fourth candidate not emerged from the interview room, he hadn't even entered it yet.

At four o'clock, the third candidate returned to the staff common room, closely followed by the head of department, who apologised for the way things were going.

"We're like a cow's tail today," he said.

Bob looked blank.

"We're all behind," was the head of department's solution to the puzzle.

At 4.40 pm the fourth candidate returned from the front, looking amused rather than shell-shocked.

"It was a farce," he said. "They asked the silliest questions."

Bob was about to seek clarification when the head of department appeared and asked Bob to follow him.

"Give 'em hell," whispered someone encouragingly as Bob stood up.

There were five members of the interview panel. They were seated on one side of a long table, and Bob was invited to take the single chair on the other side. The interviewers were sipping tea and wiping biscuit crumbs from their lips as Bob entered, but he was not offered any refreshment.

The proceedings did not start until the tea-cups and biscuit plates had been cleared away.

The chairman coughed. "Now, Mr Morgan, would you tell

us please what you think a job at Jacksbridge Polytechnic would offer you that you cannot find at Dunton."

Bob relaxed in his seat, switched his mental computer to Interview Mode, threw the switch to ON, paused for effect, and began. He knew, or thought he knew, exactly what sort of response was expected to this question, and he gave it. He had, over the years, attended a number of interviews, and the questions had not differed much. He was ready for questions on assessment of students, the problem of low motivation, the need for research activity, and the importance attached to making courses innovative, integrative, and applied.

Bob was, however, surprised when the lay member of the panel asked him what his hobbies were, but he provided the information without hesitation and that seemed to be what was needed.

At last it was Bob's turn to ask questions. The morning's discussions had prepared him well.

"I understand that you are planning to introduce a BA Combined Studies course," he said.

"Yes," said the chairman, "that is on our Forward Programme of Courses, and planning is at an advanced stage. It should come to fruition in a year or two."

"Can you tell me what the course will consist of? In particular, will it include my subject?" asked Bob.

The chairman shuffled his papers. The head of department looked awkward.

"Ah," said the chairman, "yes. A good question. A very good question indeed. But not one that I can answer definitively at this stage. Have you, perhaps, Mr Morgan, any suggestions?"

"Me? Of course not. I don't know what the object of the exercise is, nor what staff strengths you have available, nor the likely demand from students."

"Exactly, Mr Morgan, exactly. An excellent answer."

Bob was then asked to return to the waiting room, where the decision of the interview panel would be announced shortly.

All the other candidates had already returned. One was pacing up and down in the way that expectant fathers do in television comedies. It was 5.30 pm.

By six o'clock, the candidates were tired, hungry, and impatient. They had each recounted their interview experiences, and there was general agreement that a job at Jacksbridge Polytechnic was an unattractive prospect, and that the interview procedure was laughable. Bob described how he had identified that no-one knew what the BA Combined Studies degree course, whose planning was supposed to be at an advanced stage, meant. The others had found similar chinks in the armour of the opposition across the interview table.

It was not until 6.25 pm that it was announced that the post was to be offered to Bob. Everyone congratulated him. He was pleased, but only in the sense of being the winner of a tournament. He was not at all sure that he still wanted to work at Jacksbridge Polytechnic.

Bob had a meal, and then began the long drive home.

He got back to his flat at around midnight. As he parked his car, he noticed that his bedroom light was on, but it was a mistake to worry; Christine was waiting to welcome him home. Unfortunately, after a long day, she'd lost the battle, and fallen asleep, fully clothed, on his bed.

There were several letters on his bed. He noticed his mother's handwriting on one of them and, without opening it, put it straight in the kitchen bin.

Christine was overjoyed that Bob had got the job, but Bob

was less happy about this. She stayed the night at his flat. It was late and, anyway, they were going to be married.

Bob woke at 3 am and fell over Christine as he got out of bed. He went into the kitchen and retrieved his mother's letter from the bin. He opened the letter and read it. His good upbringing had won, but he quickly resolved not to let it next time. The letter assured him that its author was well and busy. The weather, it seemed, was fine. He went back to his bed in disgust, and fell over Christine again. Marital sleeping arrangements had their drawbacks.

9

The next day was uneventful, but Bob felt elated throughout the morning because he knew that he had a new job and a fiancée. He mentioned neither of these subjects to anyone because he wanted to wait until the job at Jacksbridge had been confirmed in writing, and until he had had time to talk at length to Christine. They had both overslept, and breakfast had been rushed and disorganised, and serious talk had been impossible.

By the early afternoon, however, Bob was starting to feel uneasy about his new job. The more he thought about it, the more it seemed like his present job. There seemed little point in travelling hundreds of miles and going through all the upheaval of moving to an unfamiliar town in order to be in a job with all the pressures of his present one.

Then there was the question of Christine. His thoughts on this subject were totally muddled and could not be put into words.

When Bob returned to his office in mid-afternoon after giving a lecture to first-year surveying students who attended classes in economics under duress, there was another note on his door. It said: "Please see me. KP".

"Nuts", said Bob in a loud voice, and then looked around sheepishly to see if anyone had heard.

"Come in, come in," said Ken Park as he welcomed Bob to his room, "how's the term treating you?"

"Not bad," said Bob, unwilling to commit himself.

"How did you get on in Jacksbridge?"

"I don't know the decision yet," said Bob, who felt that he needed to consider all the implications of his situation, which was beginning to seem, to him, much more complex than it was. "But," he added brightly, "it was a most interesting day. It was useful to see another polytechnic from the inside."

"And what conclusions were you able to reach?"

"That they have the same problems as we do."

"Ah yes," said Dr Park, who didn't want Bob to explain in detail. "Now the reason I asked to see you is this. You're probably aware that there is to be an institutional review in a year's time."

"Yes," said Bob. The Principal had sent a memo to all members of the academic staff about the quinquennial review, by the Council for National Academic Awards, of Dunton Polytechnic. This was the usual supplement to inspection of individual courses.

"Well," said Dr Park," a document is being prepared on the development of the polytechnic since the last institutional review."

"Yes," said Bob, "I am aware of the usual procedure."

"Oh good. Well, I've written a first draft of the description of the non-teaching activities of this department, and I'd like you to read it and send me a note of your comments."

Bob brought his mind to full attention. In view of what had happened to his last list of comments, he was not happy about putting anything in writing.

"Why me?" he asked.

"Because I know you are a man of good judgement. Which is why I'm asking everyone else in the department too."

"This is very expensive in man-hours. Are you sure it's worth it?"

"Oh yes. This is a very important matter. Anyway, here is the draft document. Would you take it away and consider it?"

Bob took the document but did not rise from his seat.

"Since it's not very substantial ..." began Bob, but saw the look on his head of department's face and began again. "I'm sure it's substantial in content, but since it's only two pages, could I perhaps read it now and give you my comments immediately?"

"Er ... yes," said Dr Park hesitantly.

Bob started reading. He smiled from time to time as he read through the two pages. His spontaneous reaction was to describe the draft document as a work of fiction, but he knew that this would be unwise.

"You've certainly painted a very rosy picture," said Bob.

"Yes, well, I've tried to emphasise the good aspects."

"The trouble is," went on Bob, encouraged by the admission that the document was misleading, "that I'm not sure you've been entirely fair."

Ken Park's face showed that he was hurt, but Bob was now ready for battle, and went on, undeterred.

"I simply don't recognise this department from your description. It's so misleading as to be almost untrue. This section on Research Activity, for example. Is it really fair to state: 'There exists a healthy research base in the department. A number of research projects are in progress and members of staff publish their results in academic journals.' What is a research base anyway? How do you measure its health?"

Ken Park tried to answer but couldn't find the words, so Bob continued.

"You say that there are 'a number' of research projects. What number do you have in mind? Two? One? Or zero perhaps? And these publications you refer to: is the *Dunton Herald* an academic journal?"

Ken Park shuffled in his seat.

"Can I make a suggestion?" asked Bob.

"Of course."

"Right. I suggest that you rewrite this section to the effect that there is very little research activity in the department and explain that one of the reasons for this is pressure on resources. In other words, people are grossly overworked. We haven't enough staff in the department to do our teaching effectively, so we need a lot more if we are expected to do research too. Either that or, of course, we could close some of our courses. Do we really need the BA in Economics? Or is it just an unnecessary burden? It doesn't attract many students, and a significant proportion of those that do enrol are not highly motivated."

Bob paused for breath. Ken Park shook his head slowly.

"You've no idea," he said, "you've really no idea at all about writing CNAA review documents. No-one tells the whole truth. We must not give the review team any excuse to withdraw validation from our courses. You've a lot to learn."

"You asked me what I think," said Bob, "and now you know."

"I wonder if you'll ever grow up," said Dr Park.

BOB WOKE EARLY the next morning. He couldn't get the Jacksbridge job off his mind. The postman called during Bob's breakfast, and one of the letters for him was a written offer of employment from Jacksbridge Polytechnic. To Bob's annoyance, he was being offered only a very modest increase in salary, and the detailed conditions of employment specified that, despite his four years lecturing experience, he would be subject to a probationary period of two years. Together these constituted the final insult for Bob, even though he knew that salary scales were agreed nationally and could not be varied by an individual polytechnic, and that probationary clauses were rarely invoked except in the most extreme circumstances.

Without further thought, he sat down at his desk and wrote a short letter withdrawing his application for the post of Lecturer in Economics at Jacksbridge Polytechnic. He immediately felt cleansed, and set off for work feeling much happier than he had the previous evening.

Having posted the letter he suddenly felt that this might have been a mistake, and then shrugged off this mood. The die was cast now, and could not be uprooted (whatever that saying really meant). During the day he told his friends that he had been offered the job at Jacksbridge and had turned it down. No-one could understand why he had withdrawn his application, or at least they pretended not to understand. Several of his colleagues had applied for the same post but had not been shortlisted, and they were particularly irritated. It was generally felt that anyone who is not going to accept a job should not apply for it, especially as, in so doing, he may keep someone else off the interview list.

By the end of the day, Bob had explained his decision so

many times that he could describe his feelings before, during, and after the interview with great fluency. The process had also convinced him that he was right not to accept Jacksbridge Polytechnic's offer. He had, however, begun to worry about ever solving his job problem. This was the first new job he had been offered since moving to Dunton; it hardly seemed an appropriate expression of gratitude to turn it down.

Bob called at Christine's flat for supper. She was very pleased to see him but abruptly released him from her welcoming hug when he told her about his letter to Jacksbridge.

"Why? For God's sake, why? You've been looking for a job for years and years. So why turn it down? Even if it's no better than Dunton, at least it would be a change." She paused for breath, but Bob wasn't quick enough on the draw, and she started again. "But what really hurts me is that you wrote that letter without discussing it with me. I am your fiancée; or had you forgotten? And what does that mean? I'll tell you what it means; it means sharing things, sharing everything. It especially means sharing decisions that affect us both. I said I'd go to Jacksbridge with you, and I've applied for jobs there. Are you expecting me to withdraw those applications? Because I might not wish to, and won't discuss it with you." Another pause for breath, but Bob again failed to exploit the situation. "Don't look at me so limply. You've reneged on your obligations to me, and you haven't even apologised!" Bob tried to apologise, but there was not time before Christine started again. "Just go home, will you, and I'll talk to you again tomorrow."

"But, Christine ..." said Bob, participating at last, even if only in a minor role.

"Out!" said Christine.

"But, Christine …"

"I said 'Out' and I meant 'Out'! Now!"

Bob conformed. He drove home. He telephoned Christine's flat, but there was no reply. He felt wretched. He didn't know if his engagement was still on. He didn't know if he wanted it to be still on. He felt totally alone, and wanted Christine with him.

He dialled her number again. This time she answered, but rang off when she recognised his voice.

A few minutes later, the telephone rang. He leapt to it.

"Hello Christine," he shouted with joy.

"No, love, it's not your Christine. It's Mrs Lowson."

Bob felt faint.

"Yes, Mrs Lowson," he said.

"Something terrible has happened, and I don't know what to do. I dare not leave my flat. Will you come around and help me?"

"Of course," said Bob, irritated and intrigued at the same time. This sounded more interesting than Mrs Lowson's usual worries, and would make a very welcome relief from Christine's tantrums.

Mrs Lowson ushered him into her flat and through into her kitchen.

"Look," she said, pointing at the ceiling.

Bob looked, but couldn't see anything unusual. He didn't know what he was looking for. Then he jumped when a drop of icy water hit his forehead.

"There!" said Mrs Lowson in triumph, "that's the problem. Can you fix it?"

"Me?" said Bob. "I'm not a plumber. You've got a burst pipe, and that's a job for an expert."

"Couldn't you just have a go?" said Mrs Lowson.

"No, certainly not," said Bob. "I wouldn't know where to

begin, anyway. But I'll phone a plumber for you."

"I'm disappointed in you," said Mrs Lowson.

"Look here," said Bob in some exasperation, "there are many problems in this world that I cannot solve, and most of them I'm not even willing to worry about. Your burst pipe is one of those. Life is too short to worry about everything, and your burst pipe is neither my responsibility nor within my abilities. But I will, if you wish, phone a plumber for you."

"I can make my own phone calls, thank you very much, Mr Morgan."

"Please yourself," said Bob, as he left her flat.

As he re-entered his own flat, Bob had a sudden thought. Suppose Christine, in her old age, turned into another Mrs Lowson. He wondered if there was any way of forecasting this. There was no doubt that Christine was already showing occasional Lowsonian tendencies. This was something to consider very carefully indeed, especially as he had not yet bought an engagement ring.

Bob went to sleep early that night and dreamed amazing dreams.

At three o'clock in the morning, the front-door bell rang. Bob woke with a jump. At first he thought that the sound of the bell had been part of his dreams, then he heard it again.

He hesitated before opening the front door. He was dressed in a very tatty pair of pyjamas that he had been meaning to replace for some time, and was in no mood to welcome visitors. Then he heard Christine's whisper: "Bob, please let me in."

He opened the door, and a sobbing Christine fell into his arms. "Bob, I'm sorry. I was so horrible to you."

Bob suppressed his spontaneous reaction, settled Christine in an armchair, and went to make her a hot drink. Marriage would require very careful thought indeed.

10

By general consent, but without any kind of formal decision, Bob and Christine's relationship returned to the *status quo ante*. They continued to see each other frequently, but no longer talked about marriage or an engagement. They both felt that this was the course of greatest benefit and least stress. Bob, in particular, was relieved; engagement had been more effort than it was worth. The main thing was that he still had Christine near when he needed her, but without the oppressive sensation of long-term commitment.

Christine withdrew her application for a job in Jacksbridge, but didn't tell Bob until after she had done so. Bob was delighted, as he had half-expected her to move to Jacksbridge and leave him marooned in Dunton out of spite. He ignored the impulse to protest, as a matter of principle and in retaliation, that he had not been consulted. After all, hadn't Winston Churchill said that in victory one should show magnanimity? And, although he had thrown away his engagement to Christine by being hasty, he did feel a sense of victory. It was one of the perversities of life.

Christine had also withdrawn her application for a senior post in Hamberbury, and Bob found this especially moving. It was a job in which Christine had expressed particular interest as the school was experimenting with some of the methods she had advocated in one of her publications. He was, however, restrained in his expression of thanks to her for turning down the opportunity of promotion in Hamberbury as he had no wish to trigger off a reaction he could not control.

ONE WEDNESDAY MORNING the following month Bob was summoned to Ken Park's office.

"Have you any plans for this evening?" he asked.

Bob hesitated; he considered the question to be an impertinence, and was unwilling to discuss his personal affairs with his head of department. Dr Park was, however, unhampered.

"That's good," he said, assuming an answer despite having allowed barely enough time for one. "What I want you to do is this. There's a Careers Convention at Birchingly this evening at 7.30 and I want you to be our departmental representative. You know the drill; you've done it before. Is that OK?"

"It's very short notice," said Bob tentatively.

"Yes, I know. And I'm sorry. Very sorry. But Roger Paterson, who was going to do it, has been taken to hospital with appendicitis. I'm asking you because you don't have a wife or children, so it's easier for you to take on these things than it is for most members of staff."

"I don't think my domestic arrangements should affect the way I am treated by my employer," said Bob with considerable feeling.

"Of course. Of course. No question of that, of course. You're absolutely right. I'm asking you because I am sure that, as a man of experience and good judgement, you're the best one for this particular task."

"I hope it will be remembered that this work is beyond my contractual obligations to the polytechnic," said Bob, who wanted to make it clear that he knew this. Dr Park certainly knew; many of his staff rigidly refused such evening duties.

"Yes, yes, of course."

"Right, then. I'll do it," said Bob, who feared that if he refused it might be quoted, out of context and not in his presence, in evidence against him. He also hoped that he might be able to refer to this incident if there was at any time a further allegation of inflexibility.

"Now please remember what is expected of you," said Dr Park. "Your job is to recruit students for the BA in Economics. Any student with the slightest interest in the subject area should be encouraged to follow it up. We get hundreds of applicants for the BA in Accountancy so anyone dithering about that course should be pushed towards the economics degree. And do be positive about the facilities of the polytechnic."

"I shall not tell any lies," said Bob.

"No, no, of course not. I didn't ask you to. But you should, please, be selective about the truths you tell."

AT LUNCH-TIME BOB telephoned Christine's school to tell her that he wouldn't be eating with her that evening. He told her what he would be doing, and why. She said she sympathised, but sounded as if she didn't mean it.

"You'll be able to get on with some writing," said Bob.

"But I want to see you," said Christine.

BOB ALLOWED plenty of time for the drive to Birchingly. It was the kind of road that motoring magazines describe as "unimproved", and he wanted to be able to negotiate the bends and the narrows without rushing.

Birchingly High School was in the main street of the town. It was built of stone with church-like windows. A diamond-shaped panel above the main door said: "Borough of Birchingly AD 1892". The interior had that special smell unique to schools: a mixture of chalk dust and unwashed feet.

Bob carried his apple box full of glossy pamphlets up the steps. He was greeted by a senior teacher wearing a faded gown and holding a clipboard.

"Dunton Polytechnic Economics Department? Yes ... here we are. It's Mr Paterson, isn't it? You're in Room 26. Down the corridor, second left, up the steps, bear right, and it's on your left."

He gave Bob a lapel-badge marked "R. Paterson".

"Actually," said Bob, "my name is Morgan. I'm standing in for Roger Paterson, who's in hospital."

"Yes, well, never mind about that," said the senior teacher. He was already directing the new arrivals.

Bob found Room 26 slightly quicker than last year. The room was twice as high as it was long. All the windows were above shoulder height. The desks, many of which were heavily engraved, were arranged in rows. Many had heavy iron frames and might have dated from the foundation of the school.

Bob cleaned a crude map of Australia off the blackboard, and wrote in big white letters: "Dunton Polytechnic – Department of Economics". He then pinned up a brightly coloured poster that read: "Dunton Polytechnic for a choice of opportunity and the opportunity of your choice" above carefully posed photographs of students listening to a lecturer, performing laboratory experiments, and enjoying a Saturday dance. He arranged his pamphlets in neat piles, pulled the front row of chairs closer, and sat down at the teacher's desk.

Five minutes before the doors were due to be opened to the public, a gowned teacher looked into Bob's classroom and told him to put his badge on.

"It hasn't got my name on it ..." Bob started to explain, but was waved aside.

"Don't make excuses, young man. Just wear it."

Bob did as he was told.

AT HALF PAST SEVEN, the main doors of the school were thrown open. No-one entered, as the street was empty. It was another twenty minutes before parents, some accompanied by their offspring, started to arrive. Each was greeted effusively by the head teacher, and handed a list of Visiting Consultants, with details of their fields of interest and locations in the building. Bob would have been amused had he known that he had been promoted to the status of Visiting Consultant. It was the kind of joke he enjoyed sharing with Christine.

After a long wait, Bob welcomed his first customers (or clients, perhaps) to his classroom. Mother and Father removed coats and hats and scarves and sat down on the chairs he had placed around his desk. Jimmy, who was looking bored already, was told sternly to pay attention, stop picking his nose, and take his hands out of his pockets. Only after another five minutes did it become apparent that they had arrived in the wrong room. They wanted Electrical Engineering, and were surprised that Bob knew nothing about this. Showing considerable irritation, they gathered up bundles of outdoor clothing, took a few copies of the BA in Economics pamphlet ("just in case"), and left the room.

Bob stretched out his legs, closed his eyes, and thought of Christine. He awoke with a jump when the next clients arrived.

"My daughter wants to do Economics."

"No, I don't. I want to do Sociology."

"I've told you again and again. There's no future in that."

"You don't know that. What do graduates in Sociology do then?"

"Never you mind. Nothing that's good enough for my daughter."

"You're mixing up Sociology with Social Work."

"No, I'm not."

"Yes, you are. And what's wrong with Social Work anyway?"

Bob coughed to indicate his presence. Three pairs of eyes looked at him in surprise.

"Can I help?" said Bob. "I'm from the Economics Department at Dunton Polytechnic. We have degree courses in Economics and in Accountancy, both of which include an element of Sociology."

"That sounds interesting."

"No, it doesn't. I want to do a specialist degree in Sociology."

"Can I suggest," said Bob, "that you take one of each of these pamphlets and go away and think about what questions you want to ask me."

"Thank you, Mr Paterson." said the mother of the would-be Sociology graduate, who had until now taken no part in the discussion. She was already looking thoroughly buffeted by shock-waves from husband and daughter, so it didn't seem worth correcting the name.

The next client was a man of military bearing who entered the room alone.

"I'm wondering where to send my son for a good education for business," he said.

"Well," said Bob, "at Dunton Polytechnic we have degree courses in Business Studies and in Accountancy that may be of use. There's also a degree course in Economics."

"Good. Good. Splendid. Sounds good. Can I have some information?"

Bob gave him some pamphlets, and his visitor looked at some of the misleading photographs.

"Looks like the kind of place I could send my son to. He'll probably fail his "A" Levels – do you take much account of that sort of thing?"

"Yes, of course we do. The entrance requirements for our degree courses are the same as for those at universities."

"Good God! You don't mean that, do you?"

"Yes, I do."

"Good God! Doesn't look like I shall be sending my son to your college after all."

Bob didn't like the use of the word "send", so tried to clarify things. "If your son would fill in one of these application forms, and put it in the post ..."

"I wouldn't trust him to take an application form seriously. I'll do it."

Bob winced. "How does your son feel about the courses at Dunton Polytechnic?"

"Not interested. Not interested at all. Just wants to be a rally driver. Has ambitions about driving across the Sahara.

But a few years at your college should put a stop to that sort of nonsense."

"Er ... yes," said Bob.

ONLY ONE OF Bob's fourteen clients that evening had what he regarded as a sensible approach. The discussion was led by a sixth-former who had clearly found out about Dunton Poly-technic, and lots of other places, and wanted to clarify a number of specific points about course content, admission requirements, and likely employment prospects. His parents provided discreet encouragement and guidance. At the end of the quarter-hour session, all three thanked Bob copiously and courteously. He's just the kind of student we won't get at Dunton, thought Bob with a wry smile.

At 9.30 the doors of Birchingly High School were closed, and the Visiting Consultants gathered together their posters and their pamphlets. Bob left half of his stock behind; he didn't want to be criticised by Ken Park for distributing too few. He declined the offer of tea and biscuits with the head-master, and set off, feeling weary, for Dunton.

BOB CALLED at Christine's flat on his way home.

"How did you get on?" she asked, bringing him a cup of cocoa.

"It was laughable," said Bob, "but I enjoyed it. I was asked a lot of silly questions by misinformed people, many of whom were not really interested in the answers. At least I know that I disobeyed orders and told the whole truth. One man thought economics was a branch of mathematics, and another confused it with electronics. Some parents think that they can bully their children into becoming academic students, and others choose polytechnic courses because they think we welcome "A" Level failures. Many of the parents showed no interest in what their children said or even in what they wanted to do. Some of the children regarded their parents with contempt and I can see why. A mad evening, but at least it'll be a year before I have to do it again."

"Bob," said Christine after a silence, "do you think we should consider getting engaged again?"

Bob's heart sank.

"Let's not talk about that now," he said.

"All right," said Christine, "if you think that's best."

"I do," said Bob.

"All right," said Christine. "I love you anyway."

Bob was silent. He had drifted to sleep in his armchair.

THE NEXT MORNING, Ken Park asked Bob how things went at Birchingly High School.

"It was an interesting evening," said Bob cautiously.

"But did you recruit any students for next year?"

"Difficult to say. Nothing definite of course, but we should get a few applications out of it."

"Good. Good," said Ken Park.

If only you knew, thought Bob.

IN BOB'S pigeon-hole was a letter from the editor of the *British Review of Banking*. He opened it in the corridor and, to the surprise of the people around him, shouted "Eureka!". His article on the latest Bank of England measures had been accepted for publication. Success at last!

THAT EVENING he showed the letter to Christine and discovered that it was not as favourable as he had at first thought. The editor described his article as "interesting and pertinent", and said that it would be published "as soon as space becomes available".

"That's not a binding commitment," said Bob. "Supposing space never becomes available?"

"Stop worrying," said Christine gently, "and be grateful for what you've got. He's only covering himself in case he has to delay printing your work. Why don't you telephone him and see if he'll say when the article is likely to appear in the journal?"

"Right as usual," said Bob with a smile.

11

———

The next morning Bob telephoned the editor of the *British Review of Banking*. He used the telephone in the departmental office since there wasn't one in his room, but this meant speaking against a background of type-writer noise.

"Hello," said Bob when the right man was eventually brought to the telephone, "this is Robert Morgan, Dunton Polytechnic. Thank you for your letter."

"Sorry, can't hear you. Bad line, I'm afraid. Speak up please."

Bob tried again, louder. "Robert Morgan, Dunton Poly-technic. Got your letter yesterday. I'm pleased you like my article."

"Good. It should appear in print sometime this year or next."

"Could you be more precise than that? When are you expecting it to be published?"

"Couldn't say. Couldn't say. Depends on how much stuff we receive, and how much of it is high priority."

"But you will definitely print my article soon?"

"I haven't given you an absolute promise, old boy, but I am anticipating that it will be published sometime. Is that good enough?"

"It's not what I was hoping for."

"It's the best I can do."

"Well, thanks anyway."

EARLY THE NEXT WEEK, Bob received a letter which he found most encouraging. It was from Henry Greig, chairman of the Association of Practitioners in Economic Statistics. It read:

"Dear Mr Morgan,

I understand from Brian Price, editor of *Economic Issues Quarterly*, that he has recently returned a typescript to you. I haven't seen your article, but from Brian's description it sounds just the thing we need for the APES conference. Would you be willing to present a twenty-minute talk describing your work? We are hoping to have the proceedings of the conference published as a book.

Please let me know your decision within twenty-four hours as we are running behind schedule.

With best wishes,

Yours sincerely,

Henry Greig"

Bob's reaction was to telephone Christine's school to tell

her, but she was with a class and could not be interrupted. He then telephoned Henry Greig to accept his offer. He also asked the date of the conference, as this vital piece of information had curiously been omitted from the letter.

Things were getting better at last. Several weeks (at least two, anyway) had passed since the last row with Christine, the *British Review of Banking* was probably going to publish his work, and he had been invited to present a paper at the annual APES conference.

Without delaying, he obtained a copy of the appropriate form, and applied for permission to be absent from the polytechnic in order to attend the conference. The bureaucrats needed lots of time to process forms.

BOB'S HEAD of department was impressed that he had been invited to present a paper at the APES conference.

"How did you get involved?" asked Ken Park.

"Once you've had work published in a journal like the *British Review of Banking*, which is widely read in the economics profession, people have heard the name," said Bob with a smile.

"You've published work too?"

"Oh yes," said Bob.

"I WAS SURPRISED to hear that you'll be speaking at the APES conference, Bob," said Roger Paterson, now fully recovered from appendicitis, "I thought you disliked the mathematical and statistical approaches to economics."

"I do," said Bob, "but the conference organisers don't seem

to know this. I hope I can keep up the deception. I'm worried about the other participants. I have a persistent nightmare about the questions at the end of my talk; I'm worried I won't even understand the questions, never mind know the answers."

"You'll think of something. You usually do."

"Thanks," said Bob.

THE CONFERENCE WAS HELD at Southbenton Polytechnic. Bob received a copy of the conference programme the day before he left Dunton, but did not read it until he was in his hotel bedroom the evening before the first day of the conference. He was disappointed to find that unlike most of the material to be presented, his paper was not summarised, but was listed with ten others under the heading "Other Short Papers". He found that he was to give his talk during the afternoon of the second (and last) day of the conference, and this was a disappointment too. What was much more worrying was that the titles of the other papers meant very little to him; they dealt, as he should have expected at a conference organised by APES, with statistical methodology rather than with economic issues.

THERE WERE about fifty participants at the conference, and it was held in a room with forty seats. The welcoming speech by the Principal of Southbenton Polytechnic was delayed for ten minutes while more chairs were brought in and placed a long one wall. They were stacking chairs with moulded plastic seats. Bob found that their shape had little in common with his anatomy. Within twenty minutes he had backache, and not long after that he felt he might be developing bed-sores.

The welcoming speeches didn't take long – not more than an hour – and then it was the specialist lectures. Bob's fears were justified; the first lecture was incomprehensible. So was the second, and the third. By lunch-time, Bob felt punch-drunk. Not only did he not understand what the lecturers said, he didn't even really know what they were talking *about*. One thing was quite certain; it was not his subject that they were lecturing on. But, he kept reminding himself, this was a conference of *statisticians*, not of economists, and his invitation to speak was no more than an accident.

Most of the lecturers had prepared slides to illustrate their talks, but these, far from helping, made things worse for Bob. To be shown a closely-packed page of algebra, heavily splattered with Greek characters, meant little, especially if there was insufficient time to read it before it was replaced with another similar page.

During the afternoon Bob gave up even trying to follow the lectures, and only his plastic chair prevented him from falling asleep.

By the second day of the conference, Bob was gaining some comfort from the fact that the audience was becoming restless. He hoped this meant that other people were as baffled as he was, but he realised that it might have been related to the lack of ventilation, or the uncomfortable seating. It might even indicate that the lectures were too elementary, though he tried strenuously to ignore this possibility.

When it was his turn to speak, Bob mounted the platform, stood at the lectern and, unlike the other speakers, waited for silence. His rule at Dunton was never to start speaking until there was absolute silence, and he saw no reason to change that at the APES conference.

"Do make a start, Mr Morgan," said the conference chairman, after a minute had elapsed.

"I'm waiting for silence," said Bob.

"Ah, yes," said the conference chairman, looking uneasy.

Eventually there was near-silence and Bob began. To his intense surprise, people listened. Some even started taking notes. It was only after the end of the conference that he found out that, for many members of the audience, his was the first interesting lecture at the conference.

At the end of his talk, questions were invited. A man at the back of the room stood up and started speaking. It was a lengthy question, verging on a lecture in itself. It lasted for several minutes. Bob quickly lost the thread of what the man was saying, but he was greatly encouraged when he saw the conference chairman looking puzzled too.

Suddenly, without making it clear to Bob whether an answer was expected, the questioner sat down.

The chairman looked at Bob.

"Mr Morgan?"

"Yes," said Bob, with only a short hesitation, "a most interesting contribution. I have a lot of sympathy with your point of view, but I'm not sure that the APES conference platform is the most appropriate place to discuss these issues. I'd rather deal with matters of elucidation at this point, and leave discussion of wider matters until after the conference proceedings end."

"Thank you, Mr Morgan," said the chairman, "I entirely agree."

~

AFTER THE TENTH of the "Other Short Papers" came the chairman's closing address. Then people stood up and drifted, chatting, out of the room. While Bob was making his farewells to people he had met in Southbenton, he was approached by a man who looked very familiar, but whose identity he couldn't place. Then suddenly he realised who it was. It was Professor Baxter, whose assistant he had been at Northleigh University.

"Congratulations, Bob, very well done," said the professor warmly, "I really enjoyed your paper. It's basically a tedious topic, I'm sure you will agree, but you almost made it come alive. By leaving out the statistical jargon and concentrating on the economic aspects, you made it into the only worthwhile item in the whole conference. I had no idea you had such a flair for public speaking. Well done."

"Thank you." said Bob, "thank you very much." He didn't like to explain that the statistical material which he had omitted was not just boring but, to him, without meaning.

"Now," continued the professor, "I have a proposition to put to you. Would you like your paper to be published in *Economics Today*, of which I have recently become the editor?"

"I would be delighted, of course," said Bob, taken by surprise, "but there may be copyright matters to be sorted out. I understand that the proceedings of this conference are to be published as a book, so you may need the agreement of APES and their publisher."

"Damn," said Professor Baxter.

BOB CALLED at Christine's flat on his way home from Southbenton. He knew it was too late for social calls, but Christine was the one person he wanted to tell about the conference and, in particular, about Professor Baxter's comments.

"Come on in," said Christine, as she stood, yawning, in the

doorway in her nightie, wiping sleep from her eyes. "I wasn't expecting to see you, but you're always welcome."

Bob went into the kitchen and made them both a hot drink. He was beginning to regret calling on Christine at such an unsocial hour, as she had not sounded quite as welcoming as she had tried to sound. Perhaps it was a bit cruel to wake her up like that; after all, no-one was dying.

He took the drinks through to her bedroom and related some of the events at Southbenton. To start with, she smiled and laughed when he did, but, after talking for a few minutes, he suddenly realised that she had become very still and quiet, and he couldn't help feeling hurt that she had fallen asleep while he was telling her one of his favourite funny stories. Still, there was no point in dwelling on such emotions, so he wrote a brief good-night message, left it on her kitchen table, and went home to his own flat to bed.

CHRISTINE PLANNED, as usual, to spend Christmas at her mother's home, and suggested that Bob should come too. He was not at all happy about this, and said so.

"Why?" asked Christine. "We are almost engaged, aren't we?"

"Um," said Bob thoughtfully, "I don't know really."

"Yes, you do, and of course we are," Christine assured him. "Look, if it'll make it any easier, I'll ask my mother to write to you. Is that OK?"

"Yes, well, it's fine. Good."

Bob was in a turmoil all day. On the one hand, he wanted to spend as much time as possible with Christine, and spending Christmas with her and her mother would be a good excuse to shorten his visit to his own mother whose behaviour and attitudes he found painful. On the other hand, visiting Christine's family surely constituted a public demonstration of an engagement (or at least a future engagement), and he didn't want that. But the counter argument to this was that surely engagement to Christine was exactly what he wanted and needed. Or was it?

12

I t was not just Christine who talked about Christmas well in advance. At Dunton Polytechnic, planning for the event took many weeks and involved a large proportion of the staff. It was not Christmas itself for which plans had to be made, but the mid-sessional examinations (or "class tests" as some heads of department insisted on calling them). Mid-sessional examinations were held for most years of most courses, but students not sitting examinations continued with their usual timetables of lectures, tutorials, and laboratory work. In some cases, students took examinations in some, but not all, of their subjects. Every year, this confused pattern generated problems of organisation, every year the hierarchy of the polytechnic resolved to devise a better system, and every year they failed to do so.

Initial decisions about the holding of mid-sessional examinations were taken by Course Committees, or on their behalf by heads of department. This process alone took many hours. The same arguments, on both sides, were voiced, and carefully minuted every year. Each year new compromises were reached which were not markedly different from the previous year's old compromises.

Once it had been decided which groups of students were taking examinations in which subjects, it then fell to the administrative staff of the polytechnic to arrange the allocation of times, rooms, and invigilators, as far as possible without disruption to students still attending their usual classes. Every year this proved to be impossible, partly because examinations occupied three-hour periods and lectures occupied one-hour periods, and partly because the polytechnic buildings were too small for the number of students and staff using them. Every examination needed a large enough room, an uninterrupted three-hour period and several invigilators, none of whom taught on that particular course. It always seemed to Bob that this was a suitable problem for the staff of the Computer Centre of the polytechnic to tackle, but evidently they thought otherwise.

Last year Bob had been his department's representative on the InterFaculty Co-ordinating Committee on Mid-Sessional Examinations, and he was relieved not to have been allocated this wearisome task again.

A different aspect of planning for Christmas in the Department of Economics related to the annual Departmental Lunch. Bob tried to keep out of this process too. Every year more than one person volunteered to organise the outing and each insisted on doing so in his or her own very distinctive way. Like the allocation of car-parking spaces, this issue aroused passions that were never evident in discussions of academic matters.

One year, Ken Park had been allowed to organise the event, and his choice had been a hotel twenty-five miles out of Dunton. Some members of the department had got lost on the way and arrived in time only to be asked for their share of the bill, and all had resented the drive afterwards. It had been generally agreed that the Christmas outing was far too important a matter to be left to the head of department.

This year, the dispute was between those who wanted a traditional meal "with all the trimmings", and those who favoured "ethnic" food at a curious little restaurant near the polytechnic whose owners advertised their expertise in Indian, Chinese, and Hungarian specialities. Bob refused to take sides whenever the issue was discussed.

A FEW DAYS after Christine had suggested it, Bob received his invitation from her mother. It said:

> "Dear Bob (Mr Morgan is much too formal),
>
> I hope you will spend Christmas with Christine and me. I've heard a lot about you, and would love to meet you. If you have other plans for Christmas, do please suggest another date for your visit to me.
>
> Hope you'll be able to come, and looking forward to seeing you,
>
> Yours sincerely,
>
> Margaret Harrison"

Bob felt that he had been cornered. He couldn't refuse the Christmas visit without arranging another date, unless of course he was willing to fall out with both Christine and her mother simultaneously, which was far too much to contemplate. He sat down at his desk and wrote accepting the invitation, and followed this with a short note to his own mother, explaining that his usual Christmas visit would be curtailed this year. This cloud certainly had a silver lining.

THE DEPARTMENT OF ECONOMICS DECIDED, by a narrow majority and with Bob abstaining, to have a traditional Christmas lunch. There was some talk of the defeated minority organising their own "alternative" meal, but the threat was ultimately not carried out.

ONE MORNING BOB arrived at his office to find coils of electric cable on the floor and an electrician drilling a hole in the wall.

"Oh good," said Bob with enthusiasm, "a telephone at last. I've wanted one since I started work here."

"No," said the electrician, "my instructions say nothing about telephones."

"What are you doing then?"

"I'm putting in computer terminals in all the offices on this floor. Next month we're doing the same on the floor below."

"But that's ridiculous," said Bob. "I don't want a computer terminal. I never use the computer. But I would make good use of a telephone. This must be costing thousands."

"That's right."

BOB MADE an appointment to see his head of department.

"This is an absurd waste of resources," he said, "there are

lots of higher priorities. Most members of this department will never use the new equipment; they don't know how to."

"You're possibly right as of *now*," said Dr Park, "but, in the future, who knows? Anyway, there's nothing I can do about it; it's part of the government's Technology Initiative, and that's an unstoppable force."

"This is ridiculous," said Bob, with great feeling.

"Yes, but there's nothing any of us can do about it."

"Any news about my telephone?"

"No. But I'll keep you informed."

Bob refrained from having a counter-productive last word.

BOB WAS JUST ABOUT to leave his flat to go and see Christine when the doorbell rang. On the step stood a man holding an open suitcase containing a range of cloths, scrubbing brushes, and polishes, and supporting on his shoulders several brooms and mops.

"I'm from Wear-Well Products," he said, "may I speak to the lady of the house?"

"I am the lady of the house," said Bob with a smile.

The salesman stepped back, looking alarmed. "Sorry, didn't realise. Shouldn't have troubled you. Very sorry." And he closed his suitcase, adjusted his brooms and mops, and retreated.

Bob ran after him. "Hey! I only meant that I live alone. I am the Domestic Administrator in this flat. I buy the brooms and polishes. There is no lady here. All right?"

"Sorry. I thought you were a ..." He couldn't bring himself to finish the sentence.

Bob looked him in the eye." And what if I was? Would it matter?"

The man looked at his feet. "I just don't like the thought of ..." he began, but Bob interrupted him.

"Oh, never mind," he said in exasperation, and went back indoors to his flat. Suddenly, he hadn't the energy to attempt to educate the prejudiced. And he needed a new broom too.

THERE WAS a full turnout for the annual departmental outing. A long table had been booked at the restaurant, and there were enough seats for the entire staff of the Department of Economics. As usual, Ken Park was the first to arrive, and he sat down at the head of the table. There was a delay of a quarter of an hour before the rest arrived together. The first to approach the table sat, as in previous years, at the opposite end of the table from Ken Park, and the table then filled from that end. The last two lecturers to enter the restaurant had to sit next to the head of department. It was the same every year.

CHRISTMAS WITH CHRISTINE and her mother was, to Bob's surprise, delightful.

Things began awkwardly because Christine's mother was not sure how to refer to Bob. As she welcomed them to her house she almost kissed Bob on the cheek, and then, to avoid his embarrassment, decided not to. Bob had been steeling himself for an embrace, and was relieved, and then somehow irritated, when the event did not happen.

"I really am pleased to meet you, Bob. Christine's been telling me such a lot about you. All these months and months I've wanted to meet Christine's ... er ... Christine's young man.

And now I have." She nearly kissed him again. "Come on in out of the cold. I'll make some tea."

Bob found Christine's mother a great tonic. The only problem was addressing her by name. She wanted him to use the name "Margaret", but he felt happier with "Mrs Harrison". The compromise was not to address her by any name at all, and like most such compromises, this pleased neither party. Bob liked Christine's mother because she was prepared to listen to what he said, and was genuinely interested in what he said. His own mother showed neither trait.

After three days, Christine returned to Dunton alone, and Bob went to visit his mother. He always found these visits extremely difficult, and was so ashamed of his mother's offensive neuroses that he adamantly refused to let Christine accompany him.

"I'll have to meet her if we decide to get married," she said quietly as they parted.

"Let's think about that when the time comes," he said.

"Thanks for saying 'when' and not 'if'," replied Christine giving him a very tight hug indeed.

Bob gulped. What had he said?

After one day with his mother, Bob was exhausted. He returned to Dunton feeling depressed. Fortunately, Christine knew the symptoms, and was able to help him. Sometimes he felt totally dependent on Christine. In so many situations she seemed to be able to cope with life so much better than him.

Bob went back to work at the polytechnic a few days before the new term began as he wanted to prepare some lecture notes. He was also searching for a topic for another article. Although neither of his earlier articles had actually been published yet, he was confident that they would, *even* if this was later rather than sooner. He tried to ignore the fact that neither the APES conference organisers nor the editor of the *British Review of Banking* could give him any firm indication of publication dates, or even if his work would be published at all. Optimistic as ever, Bob prepared a new version of his *curriculum vitae*, always kept in readiness in case suitable jobs were advertised, to include the titles of the two articles under the heading "Work Accepted for Publication". He had only a few copies of this version of his *Curriculum vitae* duplicated because he was confident that he would shortly be able to change the heading to "Publications".

In Bob's pigeon-hole was a memo sent by the Principal to all members of the academic staff of the polytechnic. It read:

The Governing Body has accepted the proposal that a limited number of professorships should be designated within the polytechnic. Such professorships will carry neither specific responsibilities nor distinctive salary scale and will normally be restricted to heads of departments. Interested members of staff are invited to obtain application forms and further details from my secretary. Short-listed candidates will be interviewed by a panel including external experts in their own academic fields. The purpose of this initiative is to reflect the continuing development and status of the polytechnic and to enhance the status of those senior members of staff who have made a special contribution to the development of their subject.

Bob laughed. Then he read the memo again, and laughed

and laughed and laughed. Then he went to see his head of department.

"Have you seen this memo from the Principal?" he asked.

"Oh yes," said Ken Park, "I helped him write it. I was a member of the planning committee that drew up the proposals for professorships at this polytechnic."

"It's ridiculous," said Bob, "the whole idea is ridiculous. It not only has no merits, but it will divert energy and resources from things that matter."

"But there are no resource implications. Professorships will not attract increased pay."

"But I bet these 'External Experts' will be wined and dined."

"They will be entertained, certainly."

"And, as an economist, surely you accept that human time, especially high-salary human time, is a valuable resource? How many hours did you spend at meetings of the planning committee?"

Ken Park coughed awkwardly, and Bob felt it best to withdraw from the room without waiting for a reply. As he left he noticed a half-completed form on the desk; even though it was upside-down, he could read the heading: "Application for Professorship". That's absurd, thought Bob, they've even had special forms printed.

13

———

Bob pulled another sellotaped note off his office door. It had several rows of squiggles on it. He was about to discard it as a hoax, and then took a closer look. Could this be written in Urdu? Or Arabic? Then Bob realised why the squiggles looked vaguely familiar; the note was written in Pitman's shorthand!

He took the note along the corridor and handed it to the departmental secretary.

"Could you read this to me please?" he asked.

The secretary looked surprised. "Where did you get this?"

"It was on my office door."

"It must have been left by that typist from downstairs who was here yesterday while I went to a funeral. Silly girl! Fancy leaving a note in shorthand! Anyway, it says: 'Bob Morgan. Please telephone Elaine Bramley at the Regional Office.'"

Bob looked blank.

"Who is Elaine Bramley?"

"I don't know."

"The regional office of what?"

"I don't know."

"Where is this regional office?"

"I don't know."

"Is there a telephone number?"

"No."

"Any other information?"

"No."

"Well, that's that, then. I shall just have to wait for further instructions."

BOB'S MYSTIFICATION lasted for two days with varying degrees of intensity. Then he found another note on his door, this time in the elegant handwriting of the departmental secretary. It said: "Please telephone Elaine Bramley at the regional office of the Open University."

So that was it! Bob had completely forgotten that many months ago, at least eight and possibly nine or ten, he had applied for a part-time tutorship with the Open University. Having heard nothing – and he knew that his referees had not been contacted – he had written it off. This message sounded promising, so at the first convenient moment he went out to a bank and obtained ten pounds' worth of small coins and then went to a public telephone to make the call. He didn't want to be distracted by the noise of the departmental office, and *he* didn't want an audience either.

When he had got through to the regional office of the Open University he asked to speak to Elaine Bramley.

"She's not here today."

Bob was about to replace the receiver, but added as an afterthought: "This is Robert Morgan, Dunton Polytechnic. I was asked to telephone her."

"Oh good. I have a message here for you. Elaine says she is

hoping to offer you a part-time teaching post, and can she meet you for an interview? She suggests that she could meet you at 5 pm tomorrow at the main entrance of Dunton Polytechnic. Is that OK?"

"Yes, that's fine," said Bob.

Bob returned to the polytechnic with his pockets weighed down with several bags of small change. His telephone call had cost only a single coin.

ON HIS WAY home Bob filled the petrol tank of his car and paid with a ten-inch pile of coins.

"Have you been robbing a chocolate machine?" asked the cashier.

"Yes," said Bob, and giggled.

The cashier looked alarmed and shut the till quickly.

AFTER *THE ARCHERS*, Bob told Christine about his interview the next day and they both looked at the details of the job he had applied for all those months ago.

"It looks interesting," said Christine. "The students are adults, so they should be keen. And they'll have some general knowledge about political affairs, and that should surely be important in economics. And there's the money – you could buy a decent car."

"Watch it," said Bob, smiling. "Don't insult my next of kin. She may be old and frail now, but I remember her in her prime."

Christine hugged him. "Am I in my prime?"

"You'll always be in your prime," said Bob without feeling silly.

Bob waited at five o'clock at the main door of Dunton Polytechnic. It was not long before he was greeted by a woman in frayed jeans.

"Robert Morgan? I'm Elaine Bramley."

Bob was startled. He was expecting his interviewer to be more formally dressed.

They went up to Bob's office on the top floor. The lift was out of order, and Bob's guest was out of breath when they arrived.

"I'm not used to this kind of exertion," she said. "The regional office is all on the ground floor."

Bob made no comment. Elaine Bramley opened her briefcase, and there was an avalanche of paper onto the floor. She stuffed most of it back, but handed one sheet to Bob.

"That's the syllabus we want you to teach," she said.

Bob looked at it. It described the inter-disciplinary first-year course in the social sciences.

"Well," said Bob, trying to marry honesty with a desire to get the job, "the economics is material I already teach, so that's no problem. I did sociology and politics as subsidiary subjects in my own degree course, so I could manage them too. But I'm not sure about the geography and psychology parts of the course. In fact, I'm not sure that I understand half the words used in the psychology syllabus."

"Don't worry about that; I'm sure you'll manage. Now this *here* is the timetable of tutorials we want you to take. We're allocating you to Birchingly Technical College."

"That's over thirty miles away," said Bob.

"You'll get your expenses paid. And we might perhaps be able to transfer you to Dunton later."

"Is this a permanent contract?"

"In effect, yes."

"What does that mean?"

"It means it isn't a permanent contract; it's a 12-month contract. But we almost always renew them if the tutor wants to stay with us. Which, of course, we hope you will."

She paused for breath. "I expect you'd like to see some of the teaching material."

"Yes please."

"Right. I'll show you some units."

"What are units?"

"Sorry – Open University jargon. A unit is a correspondence text that contains one week's work. You'll find that there's lots of Open University jargon. For example, students don't write essays, they write TMAs".

"What does TMA mean?"

"Tutor-Marked Assignment. And multiple-choice quizzes in the units are called SAQs."

"What does SAQ mean?"

"Self-Assessment Question. But if multiple-choice questions are part of the assessment process then they are called CMAs."

"What does CMA mean?"

"Computer-Marked Assignment. You'll get used to all this fairly quickly. There are various forms that make the system run. You fill in a PT3 with each TMA you mark. You send in a Y16 to claim expenses, and you use a PT2 to report particular difficulties to me. Keep a record of each student's progress on a PT1, with a survey of your whole group on a PT4. There are several others but those are the main ones. You needn't worry about E39 and C39 until just before the exams. And, of course,

I've said nothing about the forms used to record handicapped students and their particular problems. Is that OK?"

"I think so," said Bob. "Have I got the job?"

"Of course. Can you start tomorrow?"

"Tomorrow! That's very short notice."

"Yes, well, sorry about that. Someone else backed out at the last minute. But you nearly got the job instead of him to start with. I don't want you to think of yourself as a second-best candidate."

"But I am, though, aren't I?"

"Only by a very tiny margin."

"Yes, I'll take the job."

"Good. Right; here's a contract for you to sign. Here's a supply of assorted forms. They're a bit mixed up but I'm sure you'll be able to sort them out. The white one on top is the one you fill in if you need more forms. Don't run out of Y16s or you won't be paid on time."

Bob felt that his head was swimming with jargon, abbreviations, and forms.

"Now", went on Elaine Bramley, "have you understood the Open University system? The students receive units through the post, but I've got yours here. I think the set is complete. You provide help and guidance at weekly tutorials. They have been sent TMA titles and submission dates, and it's your job to mark the TMAs. You send the marked scripts to us for checking and we send them back to the students. They have to attend a residential summer school, but your contract does not include teaching there. There's an application form for summer school teaching posts in this bundle of forms if you decide you want to apply. Any questions?"

"No," said Bob, who was feeling punch-drunk.

"OK then, I'll be on my way," said Elaine Bramley,

standing up. She left Bob surrounded by the contents of her briefcase.

THE FOLLOWING EVENING Bob drove to Birchingly Technical College. The classroom was still empty when he arrived, so he re-arranged the chairs in a circle. His list indicated a maximum attendance of fifteen students.

When the fifteenth person entered the room, precisely on time, he began.

"Good evening. I'm Bob Morgan, and I'm your tutor for the first-year class in social sciences."

"That's not the name I've been given," interrupted someone.

"Nor me," said someone else.

"Sh!" said all the other students.

"Another tutor had to withdraw at the last minute," explained Bob.

"Well, I hope you're properly qualified for the job," said the man who had interrupted before.

Bob was taken aback. This was not how polytechnic students addressed him.

"Yes," said Bob. "I can assure you that I am properly qualified for this job, both in terms of examinations passed and teaching experience."

The interrupter subsided, and several of the other students looked at him threateningly.

"Right," said Bob, hoping he had won the first round, "as a way of starting to learn your names, I'll read out the names on my list, and please indicate if you are here. James Anderson?"

"Yes."

"Mary Bowley?"

"Yes."

"Barbara Drury?"

"Yes."

"John Edwards?"

"Yes."

"This is just like bloody primary school", said the interrupter.

"Sh," said all the others, and Bob continued through the alphabet.

When he reached the end of his list there was one name that he had not ticked.

"You must be Mr Morton," he said to the interrupter, who had not answered to any of the names.

"My name is Norton, but it's obviously too much trouble for you people to get it right."

"Sorry," said Bob, knowing he had lost the second round.

"Now", said Bob, trying to make a fresh start, "let's begin the tutorial."

"About bloody time," said Mr Norton under his breath. Everyone else pretended not to hear.

"I've made some notes on what I consider to be the important points in Unit 1," said Bob, "but since you all will have read through this week's material at least once by now, perhaps I should begin by asking if any of you would like to suggest a start to our discussion. There may be a section of the text that you find difficult, or boring, or which you don't agree with, and I'd be happy to start from such a comment."

"Can I make a suggestion?" asked John Edwards, "I'd like you to explain the diagram on page 14."

There was a flutter of pages as everyone found the place. Bob looked at the diagram and found it completely unfamiliar. It was also incomprehensible. He must have missed that page the previous evening.

"Would anyone like to answer that?" asked Bob hopefully. He stared at the diagram and tried to make some sense of it.

"I thought you were the bloody teacher," said Mr Norton.

"I am," said Bob, "but this is a tutorial rather than a lecture, so everyone should participate. If there is a member of the class who has understood the diagram, then explaining it will help to fix the ideas in his or her mind. Equally, if someone thinks they have understood it but have not fully mastered the ideas, then trying to explain it to other students will make this clear. It's a well-established technique in higher education."

"Sounds bloody daft to me," said Mr Norton with feeling.

BY THE END of the two-hour class, Bob felt exhausted. He had tried many times to ignore Mr Norton, but he was not easy to ignore. Bob resolved to take a firmer line with him next week.

When he got home, Christine was waiting for him. He greeted her briefly and then sat down at his desk to complete the PT6 and Yl6 forms for the evening's work. Whatever else happened, he was determined that no-one would find fault with his forms.

CHRISTINE WAS SURPRISED that Bob was so tired after his first Open University class.

"The majority of the students are superb," he told her, "but there is one disruptive wretch who's twice my age, twice my weight, and half my brain-power, and I haven't found a way of dealing with him yet. Teaching at the polytechnic is a doddle compared to this. And I constantly have nightmares about the forms. There are far more of them than I was told at my interview. And that's another thing; it wasn't an interview. I feel as though I've been conscripted and then sent to the Normandy beaches without any weapons training. I don't even know whether I'm supposed to march east or south."

"Cheer up, Bob," said Christine.

"And I shall miss *The Archers* once a week too."

"Look," said Christine, "things can only get better. Remember how you found lecturing at the polytechnic to start with. You hated it."

"I was a disaster," said Bob with a smile.

"Exactly. And now you're very good at it. And don't forget that Open University work can be included on your *curriculum vitae*."

"That's true," said Bob feeling better.

"And there's the money."

"Yes," said Bob, feeling almost cured. Christine always saw things in their proper perspective. He hugged her. The therapy was complete.

14

Bob went to see Ken Park. He had been summoned by the usual means of a sellotaped note on his office door.

"Come in Bob; nice to see you," said Ken Park jovially. "Do sit down. There are two matters that I want to raise with you. First, I understand that you have taken on part-time employment with the Open University."

"Yes," said Bob, totally surprised, but also pleased, at his head of department's interest.

"I didn't give permission for you to do this work," continued Ken Park.

Bob was no longer pleased.

"No," he said, "I didn't ask permission. I don't need permission. What I do in the evenings and weekends is no concern of my employer."

"But your contract with this polytechnic clearly states ... or perhaps only implies ... or perhaps it's just a convention, I'm not sure, that you must not do anything that interferes with your work at the polytechnic."

"And in what way has my work at the polytechnic been interfered with?"

"It's a latent possibility."

Bob snorted. "Then raise it with me if it ever happens," he said firmly.

Ken Park was clearly embarrassed, but overcame it without hesitation.

"I still think you might have discussed it with me."

"It's got nothing to *do* with you."

"But you might have sought my advice. I am more experienced than you."

"Experienced in Open University work?"

"Well, no," Ken said. "I just don't understand why you insist on keeping things secret from me."

"That's absurd. It's not a secret. I do have secrets from you, of course, but you don't know what they are. And I'm not going to tell you. But my Open University work isn't a secret. If it was, you wouldn't know about it. I didn't discuss it with you not because it's a secret but because it's a personal matter which is not your concern."

"Yes, well, I ... er ... I think you've made your point."

"Are you apologising?"

"Yes, well, I ... er ... I suppose so."

"Thank you."

"Let me move on to the other item I wish to discuss with you."

"What else have I done to upset you?"

"Nothing. Nothing. There's a vacancy on a selection panel next Wednesday. We're interviewing six candidates for the vacant lecturer post in this department. Roger Paterson is ill again, and I'd like you to take his place on the interview board."

"That sounds interesting. I've never been on your side of the table during an interview."

"Of course, I'll ask Roger to do it if he's fit again by then. He's much more experienced than you."

"How am I supposed to gain experience if experience is always offered to those who already have it?"

"An amusing philosophical point."

"It wasn't meant to be amusing."

"Wasn't it? Oh well, I don't know the answer. Anyway, if Roger is not back by then, you'll join the interview board. I'll see you the day before and tell you the questions I want you to ask."

"But surely you'll be on the board too?"

"Of course."

"Then I'll devise my own questions. If you don't trust my judgement then nominate someone else."

"Yes, well ... I see."

WHEN BOB ARRIVED BACK at his office there was a neatly dressed man holding a briefcase waiting there.

"Mr Morgan? Are you free now? Can I see you for ten minutes?"

"Yes," said Bob, although he didn't want to speak to anyone except Christine at that moment.

"I'm Ian Hunter from Kennedy and Rutherford."

"I'm sorry; I haven't heard of Kennedy and Rutherford."

"We're a big American publisher of academic texts, and we're trying to establish ourselves in the British market. We already have a subsidiary company in Australia, where we've been very successful, and the Australians are nearly as British as the British, aren't they?"

Ian Hunter guffawed. Bob remained stony-faced and silent and, seeing this, his visitor stopped laughing and started talking again.

"We've a wonderful range of books in your subject for all levels of students." He opened his briefcase. "This one, for example, is ideal for first-year undergraduate courses."

He handed Bob a heavy book. Bob took it, and opened it at random. It fell open at the chapter on banking.

"This is useless for our students," said Bob, glancing at it. "All the institutional information is based on United States structures." He closed the book and opened it again, this time where it dealt with taxation. "The political information is American too. This has little relevance to Britain; the constraints are different. If other lecturers have said other-wise, they're fooling you."

"OK. OK. I take your point. But that's a complimentary copy; would you like to have it on the firm?"

"Well ...", began Bob.

"I'll put it on your bookshelf", said Mr Hunter, and did so ... Now here's a list of our other books. Can I send you a free copy of any of these by post?"

Bob glanced at the list, and it aroused no interest.

"Look," he said, "I've had a difficult day. I can't think about this now. Can I look at this list tonight and then let your office know by letter or telephone?"

"That's not how we usually do things."

"Then I don't want any of them."

"Oh dear, Mr Morgan, oh dear; not what I expect from an enthusiastic young lecturer."

"Then I'll have one of each on the list."

"That's ridiculous! There are over two hundred books listed."

"Make up your own mind what to do, Mr Hunter. I shall not be offended whatever you decide."

Bob stood up and held the door open.

"Goodbye Mr Hunter."

"Goodbye Mr Morgan, and thank you."

CHRISTINE WAS AMUSED at the Ian Hunter incident.

"If they send you lots of books and they're useless to you, give them to the polytechnic library. You'll buy goodwill without cost to yourself."

She's talking like an economist, thought Bob, and I wonder if it's my influence.

BOB WAS ENGROSSED in a pile of essays when there was a knock on his office door.

"Come in," he said, without looking up.

Martin Evans entered. Bob shuddered.

"Hullo. What can I do for you?"

"I've applied for a job in an accountant's office, and I'd like to quote your name as a referee. I decided to abandon my degree course. May I use your name?"

"Yes," said Bob, "you can quote my name. But I must warn you that I shall be strictly honest. It might be in your interest to have a word with one of the other lecturers who know you."

"No," said Martin Evans, looking glum, "I was even ruder to the others than I was to you."

"Well, you must make up your own mind what to do. You failed your first-year exams, failed the resit exams, and failed at the Appeals Board. What is much more important at this stage, however, in my opinion, is that you did not accept these decisions with good grace. You were extremely aggressive and your father's letter to the Appeals Board did nothing to improve your standing."

"I know," said Martin Evans, still looking glum.

Bob began to feel very cruel. "look, I'll do what I can for you if I'm asked for a reference."

"Thank you, Mr Morgan. You're very kind."

No, I'm not, thought Bob, I'm a mug.

THE ENTIRE STAFF of the Department of Economics gathered in a classroom at 4 pm that Friday for the presentation to George Bennett, who was leaving after working for forty-one years at the polytechnic. Money had been collected over a period of several weeks and had been used to buy a leather briefcase, though it was not clear what use would be made of this in George's retirement.

Ken Park called for silence.

"May I have your attention please? It is my pleasant and unpleasant duty this afternoon to make this presentation to George. Pleasant, because it is a recognition of his many years of faithful service to the department, and unpleasant because we are sad to lose him. We wish you well, George."

There was an attempt at applause.

George stood up.

"Thank you," he said, and sat down.

There was another attempt at applause.

Ken Park stood up again. "I have a meeting arranged with the Principal, so I hope you will excuse me. Good luck to you, George."

He left the room.

George stood up. "I was hoping he wouldn't stay long. Now, in that cupboard," he pointed, "there are some refreshments, and I hope you'll join me in sharing them."

Someone opened the cupboard and brought out two dozen cans of beer, two bottles of lemonade, and three dozen sticky cakes. When everyone had started to eat and drink, George stood up again.

"Now that the boss has left the room, I can thank you properly. I'm not foul-mouthed enough to say nasty things in his presence, but I couldn't bring myself to be generous in my thanks either. But I am very moved at your kind gift and your good wishes, and I thank you for them. I've been longing to get out of this dump for years, and I shall not miss it. But I shall definitely miss the people who comprise the polytechnic. You've been good colleagues and good friends. This place has changed dramatically since I started work here. When I first came here, when it was called the Technical Institute, the students were mostly on part-time technician courses, and they were as keen as mustard. We worked the students hard, and they worked us hard. I know that sounds a rosy picture, but it's true. Today's students attend lectures to get inside out of the rain. They enrol as students because it's better than being on the dole. Now I know this doesn't apply to all the students, or even a majority, but there's enough of them to influence the general atmosphere of the place. The other thing that's changed is the complexity of the administration and paperwork. When I arrived, there were very few committees, and therefore very few documents to be written, discussed, revised. discussed, re-revised, filed, approved or rejected, and so on. The place was run by the Principal and he did it damn well, not like the present chap. I don't know why I'm telling you all this as you know it all already. Yes, I do; I want to warn you not to make the same mistake that I made. I wasted a great chunk of my life by staying here far too long. You younger men and women should get out soon, while you still can. That's all I want to say. Thanks for the gift. Who'll join me in a second beer?"

There was a spontaneous and prolonged burst of loud cheering and clapping.

WHEN BOB LEFT the classroom after George Bennett's presentation he found another note on his door. It said: "I have decided to co-opt someone more experienced, so we don't need you on the interview panel. KP."

BOB WAS VERY SUBDUED that evening. George's speech had been very moving. He told Christine about it at length. Bob had been very forcefully reminded of how unhappy he was at Dunton Polytechnic. Christine understood fully; she had seen him show increasingly severe stress symptoms, and she longed to help.

"I have decided," said Bob, after more than an hour discussing the whole problem with Christine, "to launch an all-out campaign for a new job. That must be the only way up: to get out of Dunton Polytechnic. I shall have to apply for non-teaching jobs too – higher education is a contracting industry – though I'd miss teaching desperately, and I'm not sure what other work I could do."

"What about overseas jobs?" asked Christine.

"Well, yes," said Bob, "I've never applied for overseas jobs, but if it's an all-out campaign then now is the time to start.

Yes, I shall definitely be applying for overseas jobs. I think New Zealand appeals to me, and Australia perhaps. It would be a big upheaval, though, to emigrate."

"I'd come with you," said Christine.

"Then let's buy an engagement ring in the morning."

Christine nearly smothered him with her kisses, and he knew that some of his problems were solved already.